OLD HABITS DIE HARD
The Network and Other Spies

Ret. Major David Ivor William Taylor

OLD HABITS DIE HARD
THE NETWORK AND OTHER SPIES

Copyright © 2015 Dr. David Ivor William Taylor.

All rights reserved. No part of this book may be used or reproduced by any means, graphic, electronic, or mechanical, including photocopying, recording, taping or by any information storage retrieval system without the written permission of the author except in the case of brief quotations embodied in critical articles and reviews.

This is a work of fiction. All of the characters, names, incidents, organizations, and dialogue in this novel are either the products of the author's imagination or are used fictitiously.

iUniverse books may be ordered through booksellers or by contacting:

iUniverse
1663 Liberty Drive
Bloomington, IN 47403
www.iuniverse.com
1-800-Authors (1-800-288-4677)

Because of the dynamic nature of the Internet, any web addresses or links contained in this book may have changed since publication and may no longer be valid. The views expressed in this work are solely those of the author and do not necessarily reflect the views of the publisher, and the publisher hereby disclaims any responsibility for them.

Any people depicted in stock imagery provided by Thinkstock are models, and such images are being used for illustrative purposes only. Certain stock imagery © Thinkstock.

ISBN: 978-1-4917-7917-0 (sc)
ISBN: 978-1-4917-7918-7 (hc)
ISBN: 978-1-4917-7916-3 (e)

Library of Congress Control Number: 2015953745

Print information available on the last page.

iUniverse rev. date: 10/16/2015

The End - well almost

Chapter 1

Neil stood in the sunshine and looked at the travellers who had just left the plane as he had. The money people or people who thought they had money, the less well off, wearing, plastic shoes and all of them rushing around, waiting for their luggage to be delivered. Neil stood at the back of the open to-the-air shed, a plastic roof covering a small area with two doorways, one in and one out. The latter was slightly larger than the former. Taught to be the grey man, Neil stood and waited. He was good at that. Everyone was pushing forward to the wooden tables upon which the luggage will be placed from the metal luggage trollies. This, of course, would take an age. He had seen the unloaders stop to shake hands and talk about not much with the official as he had walked down the aircraft steps to disembark.

It did not matter it was the end, well almost. After the luggage, a taxi and then walk to the safe house and in two days' time a boat out. Why not another jet much quicker, even this place had jets. He had just walked off one. Neil drifted off into his own thoughts. The last "home run", how many had he done before? He was going home to fly a desk or be a trainer somewhere. They, the mandarins, had decided for him. He was to end his time as a field officer. He wondered if his father had felt like this. There was the twist; his father had used this route for his last home run. He had never arrived in London, no body, no news agency flash, just nothing. He had boarded the plane here, confirmed, ticket everything and never arrived in London. Perhaps that was why he was on a boat. No, stick to the plan, so carefully crafted in the hotel room in Wuhan with the dark haired woman asleep in the hard double bed. Those thoughts made him forget about the plan and think about the double bed, the woman, and the time they had briefly spent together. To her he was William. That had been his father's name. In all the time, he had been in "the game" he had never previously used a name associated with his family, never. Why then, why her, why anything come to that matter? He was nearly at the end. The woman came back into his thoughts, small, petite with perfectly shaped breasts and a cute rear end. That attracted him in the restaurant in the first place. She was stopping in the hotel and en route to somewhere. Had she told him? He could not remember. Pausing in his thoughts, he looked up for the tractor and the luggage trollies. No nothing yet. He checked his watch, Skagen steel, which had been such a talking point in China, "only 6 mm thick" or some such marketing rubbish. It kept good time was not expensive and he had only needed to change the watch glass once after a fight. That was another story, yes, he rubbed his shoulder a painful story that one.

His mind drifted back to the woman, she was 51. Thankful not a girl; she had experience and was not ashamed to show it. However, she had asked him to stop after two sessions as she was "out of practice" … What would she be like if …? He stopped himself. A gentleman never discusses a lady, not even in his mind. He was smiling to himself as the tractor sound came into his hearing. He could now hear the clanking of the trollies. He, like everyone else, anxiously looked for his or her luggage. He saw the grey and red Samsonite bag at the bottom of the pile on trolley two. He stayed at the back and waited. A youngish woman with a small child was struggling with a pushchair and the child started up at him, blonde hair, pigtails a heart breaker when she grew up. He picked up his matching flight bag and moved to the wooden tables, just at the point of him going to pick up his case. A younger man pushed in front and pulled at a blue, heavy bag. No worries, he thought, the man was too busy with his luggage. He did not relax. He turned towards the door out and saw a uniformed official looking at them both. The little girl and the mother were walking past the official who was now staring in his direction. He turned back to his case and pulled it towards him, pulling off the security tag, and putting the sticker in his pocket. Neil left the luggage tag where it was, ex Beijing. Put the case on its four wheels and walked past the official, who was talking to the young man with the blue case, about where he had travelled. He came out of the secure area and passed the people offering him a taxi. He needed the toilet and quickly. He walked down the stairs and fought with the door and his cases. Inside the cubicle, he dropped his trousers and looked at the damage to his left leg. It was weeping blood again. He quickly took out the antiseptic pads and wiped the wound. Silly mistake that one, a penknife blade into his leg. Always check they are not moving before you put in the last stamp. The man, thick set, had not been moving, until he swiftly stuck a small blade into his leg. Perhaps not much for a man's last act. Yet, it had done the damage on his calf muscle and the weeping cut had been a problem ever since. He finished the first aid repair, relieved himself, and thought. Remember to pull the flush and check that the blood stained cloth flushes down the toilet. Old habits die-hard. He laughed so did he; die-hard that is. Even the doctors had failed twice with their incompetence. He slowly struggled back up the stairs, mock marble, but pretty and pushed the cases out into the bright sun light. It was hot. The cotton shirt was doing what it should do, look good and soak up the sweat. He glanced around and noticed the blonde-haired woman with short shorts and a bare midriff, long legs and a reasonable size bust, with a shirt not properly buttoned up. Never trust the ones who show too much too soon. Across the road, workers were having a break from the building renovation. The same wolf whistles when it is all on show, like that. He moved over to the taxi rank and pushed past the drivers to ask at the window how much into the town and mention the street in a poorly pronounced, but locally sounding accent. "200 the woman had said and a taxi driver picked up the big case. Neil picked up the matching flight bag and put it in the boot of the car himself. Play the tourist he thought. Showed the drive the name and sat in the back of the car, a cheap Honda, which would suit the purpose. His mobile telephone vibrated. He pulled it from his summer hunting jacket and read the message. "House is safe will meet you in the street on the corner by the café." Marianna was good and had helped him twice before when he had used this route out. Her man was something in the construction industry. What, he did not know and truthfully did not want to know. He would ring Tatiana, when he got to the apartment, well two rooms and a shower. At least, it was safe. He pushed back into the seat and watched the driver fiddling with the sat nav. Not like the old-fashioned drivers who knew where places where. Today's modern driver needed a phone, a sat nav and an unlimited supply of cigarettes and drink.

 He paid the driver and gave him as small tip. They had not spoken. He stood on the corner and wondered how was this one going to end. He was never totally lost in thought and so he noticed the girl walk past with a white zipped skirt all the way down the back from the waistband to the hem. A short white skirt, very short! Across the road the workers, who were having a break had stopped to look, as well as the wolf whistles, and crude comments followed. At that moment, a dark Mercedes stopped in front of the parked car at the roadside. He knew Marianna was not good at parking, good at driving fast, but parking was another matter. He put the cases in the back and jumped into the right hand side passenger seat. A brief kiss on the cheek and they were off into the lunchtime traffic. It was hot and the traffic was both noisy and smelt of cheap petrol, gasoil. He looked in the passenger wing mirror. No one was following. She was good, three lane changes at break neck speed and four turns that made no sense to him, but ensured no one could follow them.

"You look tired," she had broken his train of thought, which brought him back to the inside of the car. "Yes, long haul flights are not as easy as they used to be. Well for me anyway. Still this is the last one!" Neil thought to himself everyone has a point of view and shares it even if you do not want to hear it. It distracted and caused angst as everyone thought his or her point of view was relevant and should be aired, and it was.

"Really?" she asked the question. "You really are stopping the field work?" Neil grunted and looked out of the window. Who said he wanted to stop the fieldwork, some fat arsed mandarin in Whitehall, not him. No, he was wrong the mandarin was not fat arsed, was a fit young, go down the gym each morning type; who had never done a field exercise in his life. The man had most definitely never done a real mission. Still who cares, they did not so why should I? He sat and reflected not on the particular mission he was coming home from; but the last time he was at the East German border. He had been camouflaged and waiting for the guard to walk too far into "enemy" territory. He lay still in the dew soaked grass, wet and tired from the long wait. That was the one he had made a mistake when he got back home and answered his mother, when she asked him where he had been.

He replied East Germany. She launched into hating spies, game playing, she would tell them when we were overrun where a spy was, his father and now him! That marriage, to his father, had started so well, he had been told, and ended so badly. She had told him repeatedly. They ended up hating each other and she had meant ever word about shopping him to the Reds. There had even been as suggestion that she had spoken to the local known agent in the petrol station about getting him to arrange an accident for her husband. You could call the East German Guard thing an accident. It was a mucked up and Neil had the scars to prove it.

He stopped and reflected, his kneecap, his right shin, his stomach, big one that scar, and above his left eye. Not bad for eight and one half years of defending his country and himself.

The Merc pulled up outside of a small set of metal double doors. Abandoned, not parked. "The code is 72 pushed, together. Will text you if there is a problem," and then she was gone. Neil pushed the code and the metal door, inside the main door, swung open. He pushed the cases inside, climbed in over the metal frame step and closed the door. The entrance was a little tunnel with a single light bulb on all the time. Tall enough to walk through easily. He moved to the third door and opened it with the key on his key ring. On the outside it looked like any other door, good quality hard wood, inside it had fitted metal panels and Kevlar built into the fabric. Not heavy to move, but a safe door the kind you want between you and bullets. He carefully placed the two cases on the floor so as not to damage the polished surface. He moved to the kitchen opened the fridge and put some ice cubes in a whisky tumbler. Three fingers of Southern comfort, just what Doctor Neil had ordered? He never used his titles anymore. He went back outside and sat on the wooden bench. As he sat in the sun, sipping his drink a ginger stray cat came up and sat near to him. Started to clear its fur and look up into his eyes as if he knew the strange human sitting on a bench drinking booze. Life could be good sometimes Neil thought to himself, a good glass of whiskey liqueur, a rest and some sun shine. As he had moved out of the front door, Neil had unconsciously checked that the escape route door was open. Now when he looked up the door was closed. He had not done that and no one had passed him whilst he sat in the sun. The cat stopped licking its fur and stared at the metal doors, the hair on its neck standing erect. Neil looked, but could not see anyone's feet below the door. However, he was too old in the game to ignore the second sense of his newfound friend. The cat did not move. Neil put the glass on the floor and noticed some earth and dust in front of him, scuffed up as people had walked up and down the pathway to the tunnel. He heard the door click open and saw an old man slowly entering. Nothing seemed wrong, which was a good indicator that everything was wrong. The cat did not move it just kept staring. The old man seemed to shuffle and his open neck shirt blew in the wind created from opening the door. He was holding something in his left hand. That hand would be closest to Neil, when he reached him. Neil sat back no need to get anxious over nothing, until as the man came out of the tunnel Neil could see a handgun in his right hand. Neil was now thanking God for his high blood pressure and the surge of oxygen his brain was receiving. The man came closer, but was not shuffling now. Neil sat still and waited. The man stood in front of him and waved the gun for him to move. Neil bent forward and in one swift movement threw dust and earth in the man's face. He was a professional he did not try to use his hands to stop the dust, he closed his eyes for that brief moment and Neil was up from the bench. His left hand took the man's right hand and the force of the chop sent the gun flying to the ground. Neil's right hand had grabbed the man's left hand and pushed it towards his stomach. He used the man's own thumb to push the syringe as it went through the shirt and into his stomach. The man opened his eyes and as he went to move his bodily functions came out all over him and he dropped to the floor, stinking and dead. Whatever that was it was effective thought Neil. He glanced at the door and the cat was still sitting still but not looking to the metal door. It was now looking at the escape door, which was open again.

Neil never went on operations carrying anything except his issue brief case; no weapons ever, always made you a target for the police and others. However, he quickly picked up the revolver, checked the safely was off and it had bullets and stood in front of the apartment door. The wooden stairs and the balcony covered in a wooden frame were creaking. He waited again. No apparent movement, until a gun started to poke around the corner of the building. It was too low. A bullet went into the bench where he had been sitting a few moments ago. Then a dwarf rolled over and came from behind the wall by the wooden stairs. Neil fired one round into the man and he was dead. True professionals do not wait for an opportunity they take it whenever it presents itself. The mistake the first man had made.

Neil sent a text to Marianna, send a blood wagon no sirens and I am moving, have been compromised. He then rang Tatiana and said, do not come over I will be with you in half an hour. Had he telephoned her before? He could not remember. He picked up the cases as he rang for a taxi and in perfect Russian explained his needs a cab urgently for Major Olaf. The operator answered and said to wait at the corner of the road, not near the trolley bus tracks.

Bags in hand he went passed the whisky glass, picked it up and threw it to the floor, at the doorway, in smashed into pieces. It may be fingerprinted, but no one else was going to prove his fingerprints where on the outside of the glass or he had been to the safe house. Walking slowly, unhurried he passed through the metal door and out into the street, turning left he continued to the corner and moved slightly to his left away from the trolley bus tracks. A Zil made military vehicle arrived and a driver opened the door from inside. He got in. The vehicle sped off and Neil sat in the back quietly. The drive asked "Where to sir?" He gave instructions that the driver followed to the letter, without asking why or when.

"Jesus!" Neil said to no one, "I am trying to go home and have a break. Two bodies and it is not even teatime yet. Is this is a game, who is playing it, and why?"

"The Games a foot; but, whose game?"

Chapter 2

Marianna stood and looked at the carnage. He had been in town for just over two hours. "How does he do it?" she said out loud to no one in particular; "Doesn't carry a gun and one is shot dead and the other?" Marianna was a five foot six blonde beauty, married to the wrong person. Neil had never asked her and George had, still no crying over spilt milk. She turned back to the bodies. A shot dwarf, and a needle sticking out of the stomach of the other. The smell in the heat was not good. The doors to the entrance were fully open and filled with the ambulance. "Where was Neil?" "Who, madam?" A small, thin man in a T-shirt and jeans was waving a camera in her general direction. "Oh! No one" Marianna replied, "I want full shots, every angle before 4 today, matt in colour and black and white. Also shots of the court yard OK?" it really was not a question it was a command. She called to one of her men "why is the e door closed?" "I don't know it has not been used" came the reply.

As the camera clicked, she started to think about Neil again. They had been close, before her marriage. She would never two time. Where was he?

A man's voice asking if they could move the bodies broke her thoughts. "Yes, if the cameraman has finished. Ask him please?" The bodies were loaded and the metal doors shut again. Some of the team had remained with her. They sifted and looked for anything, a shell casing, the top of the syringe. There had been nothing in the pockets of either man. Marianna took the spare apartment key from her key ring and opened the door. At first glance, he had not gone into the apartment. Wait and check the fridge. Yes he had, ice cubes missing, and one glass. Where was it? She did not seen anything in the courtyard. She stopped; she had seen broken glass by the entrance. Her mobile rang; hurriedly she answered and called Neil's name. "It's me love who is Neil please?" "Oh! Sorry someone in the office who should have rung me. What's wrong darling?" "You promised me lunch and it is now well passed lunch time I was worried." Good old dependable George. "I am really sorry baby there is a problem in the office and I could not get out of a meeting to ring. I am sorry, will make it up to you tonight. I promise kisses and hugs. I have to go bye." She hung up and slowly walked out of the apartment to the doors and looked for the glass, swept up and gone. Too many blanks and too many problems, she mused to herself, where is he, what kind of game was this he was playing? Was he hurt, no blood except the dead men. Marianna remembered that he had limped when going into the apartment, was he hurt, he had not said anything, where was he.

To no one in particular and every one there, she called, "Wrap it up and back to the office now please. We have some things to sort out." She moved towards the metal doors and the entrance.

"Will you require your uniform sir?" an orderly asked Major Olaf, Major Neil Olaf of the ... nobody knew, but he was a senior man. He arrived unexpectedly and disappeared just as quickly and quietly. "Just get me a strong black coffee, an espresso, if you can manage it, Eric." The orderly could not imagine how such a man could remember his name; but he had just called him by his first name Eric. He walked off to get the coffee with a spring in his step; Major Olaf had remembered his name and called him by it.

Neil turned to the special phone on his desk and dialled a number. Anyone watching would have realised that it was not enough numbers. The number rang and Neil spoke "Dobryy den" slowly and calmly Neil spoke into the handset and explained the situation. Then he asked "Khto stoyav za tsym?" (Who was behind this?)" Diznaў tesya, shvydko, yakshcho vy …" (Find out quickly if you … …) Neil's voice trailed off and he put the handset down. A knock on the door interrupted his thoughts. "Vvodit'" (Enter)

Eric marched in, smarty, with a large smile on his face and a cup of coffee in his hand.

"Malen'kiy chernyy espresso v chashku mayora." (A small black espresso in a cup Major). He left without a salute, as was the custom.

Neil picked up the special phone again and dialled another short number. "Je sortais via Paris. S'il vous plaît prendre les dispositions. Non pas, par voie aérienne bateau vous tromper." (I am coming out via Paris. Please make the arrangements. No by air, not boat you fool.). He put the hand set down and started to plan, whilst sipping the coffee. It smelt good and tasted better, hot espresso nothing better in the world to drink. His father had been an espresso drinker, according to his mother. She described him as "a real coffee drinker, no watered rubbish for your dad." He reflected upon that pretty, but bitter woman, his mother. She had been a beauty by any definition. His mother had aged badly and had hated his father, with a passion most people never achieved in their life. From the moment she had taken him by the hand as a small boy and walked out of the family home, not one good word about his father had she ever spoken? Don't you go into the game like that old fool did; seduced him better than I ever could or wanted to. She must have turned in her gave when Neil accepted the invitation to join International Knowledge Services Plc. as the finance director. After years of training and language learning, let loose on an unsuspecting world of espionage, an MIO (Military Intelligence Officer), a spy, the third in the family; his uncle Stan, who he had never met, his father and now Neil. What a family tradition! He remembered his mother's words. "If there was an Olympic event for telling lies you father would have won so many gold medals."

Neil stood up! He hoped that Tatiana was waiting for him. He needed to feel her warm body next to his and she was the lady he needed now and always. He flicked the switch and said over the intercom "Ya na nekotoroye vremya" (I am out for a while). He walked to the sidewall and pushed the light switch, the wall moved and a panel opened to allow him into the street at the back of his office. He walked out into the hot weather again with his cases. Put them in the back of another dark Mercedes and was about to drive off when he thought he saw someone's head pop out of the secret doorway. He stopped looked and could not see anyone else in the alleyway or by where the door had previously opened out. He opened the car door, sat down and waited. The door did move, as he watched it in the internal mirror. He saw Eric's head pop out, see the car and pop back in again, a bit like a jack in the box that children played with. Neil turned the engine over and moved off slowly, the gates at the back of the consulate opened up for him to pass through. He had gone to the Russian's as he felt that something was wrong with the firm. Now he felt there was something wrong with the Russians. He checked for traffic and smoothly pulled out into the flow of the early evening drivers. Tatiana would be waiting.

Tatiana was waiting, it was hot and she was dressed in matching bra and a thong, black with little red flowers. Neil liked matching underwear she knew this of old. She was worried; they had agreed to meet in London after this job. She did not know what was wrong so she put a small silk jacket over her body; loosely tied the belt and sat down again. He had not sounded rushed, but perhaps he did on the voice message. Then there was the text. She was worried.

At 54 Tatiana was in very good shape for her age, ample bust that Neil liked, he called her backside his cute rear end, no fat there yet, and a slim waist. Married twice, but no children. She had fallen for Neil the first time she saw him. He was drinking Southern Comfort in a small bar just around the corner from her office. She popped in there for coffee, snacks and to eye up the men from time to time. Well she was a woman who had needs. Neil was different, even then, straight back, broad shoulders and not much of a belly. How he hated that word belly. She wanted to smoke, but he hated that as well. She hated the way he kept her waiting; but, she loved him and he knew it. She would do anything if he were hers. At present, Neil was no ones. She was certain that there was no one else he slept with that she knew about. He said that he loved her, but nothing had come from his words yet. She heard the door of the garage open up electrically and the sound of a car engine. He was here, wonderful; she rushed to pump up the cushions, sprayed a little perfume between her breasts and waited for the door to open.

Marianna was on the verge of opening the car door and telling her number two her thoughts about the glass when someone called her name. She turned and her hand went towards her gun holster. As the second bullet hit her and she fell into a pile of broken glass. She had found the glass in her death. The team were quick to react, shooting at the man as he jumped into a dark

Mercedes and start to move away. The number two levelled his revolver and took three taps. The first broke the car windscreen the second went through the hole and into the driver; the third went through the glass and into the man's forehead. Only then did he rush to Marianna's side. She mouthed "the glass … Was here" and the breath run out of her body. The last sound on her lips was not Neil but George's name as she died in someone else's arms.

Neil arrived at Tatiana's and found himself wondered about lots of things such as Eric, about the escape door, about whomever it was using a dwarf, a possible mole in the section, who was trying to kill him. China had been safe; perhaps he should go back there? At least he should be safe with Tatiana. Safe until he could catch a plane to Paris and get the hell out of here; which in Neil's humble opinion could not be too soon after today's offering. He made certain that the garage doors were locked shut and took the cases from the back of the car, walked slowly up to the adjoining door to Tatiana's apartment. "What a day," he said to no one as he opened the door with his key.

Things that go Bump in the Night

Chapter 3

London centres signals duty officer read the message and shook his head. He misquoted John Wayne, "Things were going to be alright, if the creek did not rise; but, it had." A lifelong Wayne fanatic, Signals 2 could usually find a quote from one of the one hundred and seventy seven films. All hell was about to break free and it was always on his watch. Something was happening in the Black Sea and the Americans were on the horn and now this message about his friend of many years standing Neil being in trouble. Neil had told him this was a school run for small kids and it was fast becoming a shooting gallery. He passed the message "upstairs" and went back to the problems on the board in front of him. A Soviet destroyer in the Black Sea was bumping an American ship. Why did it always happen on his watch? Could it get much worse tonight, he wondered to himself and let out a long loud sound. The people in the room did not hear him, as they were all wearing cans. He moved to the briefing board and wrote up a list of circuits. He knew their activation sequence. He also wrote next to the list, if they are not in this order, we have trouble with a capital T. He was correct, of course, he was always right. To date he had never called an exercise, planned for conflict or war incorrectly and it was playing on his mind. If he were, wrong how many people would die? He would have missed notifying the third world war. He was getting jaded and tired of this analysis and prediction lark. He and Neil were going to set up a new research and development desk as soon as Neil returned from this home run that he had called it. He was worried that Neil might never make it home, wherever home was to Neil. Everybody knew you could get him at the Army and Navy club in Pall Mall, but that was not his home. A very nice place, Neil had taken him there for lunch once or twice, the food was good, and the place was the image of an officer's mess, simply the only place to stay when in London Neil explained as they eat their lunch together. A buzzer sounded and Sigs 2 went into action. "Signals desk 2 speaking how may I help you? Duty officer speaking! An American drawl sounded on the end of the line. "Hey Charles, how is life in merry old England?" Only an American could come over as that silly. A bit, like what is the weather like when it is four o'clock in the morning and you cannot see anything outside. "We have a small problem with your assessment, old buddy." "May I take you name please; I am Sigs 2 duty officer." "Yes, yes sorry DDSigs1A here, old boy. Are you sure of your assessment? Are the circuits going to come up in that order? Are you sure? "Yes I am sure. If not one of them comes up like that, we will have to watch for the star formation at Odessa. If that comes up we will have trouble as well as world war III." There was a stunned silence on the line before DD Sigs1A; "old boy" came back with "you serious?" "Never more so, my country cousin!" He heard a muffled "oh shit" and the receiver go down.

Whilst this was happening in London, the situation in Odessa was getting worse. Another shooting, the third shooting at the address and the police were all over the place like flies on a dung heap. Asking a barrage of stupid questions, which were directed at Maurice and he did not like it.

"Who shot the woman,"
"The man in the passenger seat of that car."
"With what?"
"A gun!"
"Who shot the men in the car?"
"I did!"
"With what?"
"A gun, my gun. Here is my licence to possess a fire arm."
"Where are the guns now?"

The number two, called Maurice, was fed up with this fiasco. He needed to be back at the office and sorting things out, not standing on a street talking to some fool of a police officer. He broke into fluent Ukraine "my zaynyati pryvatnymy, derzhavnymy zareyestrovanykh okhorontsiv, khto prosto dayťe ïkh bosa vb'yut'. Bud'-yaki problemy, bud' laska, zatelefonuyťe na tseў nomer." (We are privately employed, state registered bodyguards, who have just let their boss be killed. Any problems please ring this number.) The police officer looked at the number and realised that it was the telephone number of his boss. How did he? He gave up and said to his team to clear out and let them go.

Maurice got behind the wheel of the car, slipped the clutch and drove away too quickly for the liking of the police officer. The firm had already picked up Marianna's body and taken it to the local mortuary. Maurice needed to let George know what had happened. Maurice did not want George to see him hot, bothered, and smelling of gun smoke. He needed to break it gently to him as he talked about his dead wife. Maurice and George always made an effort when they were together, cut and clean fingernails, toilet water and decent aftershave. They had been lovers since before Marianna and she did not know. Now she was dead and George would need Maurice even more. Well that was what he thought as he drove towards George's flat, not to the office. He turned left into a stream of traffic and headed for the flat.

Neil walked up the stairs from the garage and looked out of the window at the street below. No parked cars, a couple kissing outside a shop. The shop was closing up; the streetlights were just coming on. The couple parted and the man looked just like Eric. It could not be, could it? It really did look like Eric from the consulate. Yet Eric had neither a car nor the ability to follow him. Unless he knew the apartment, but how? Neil carried on up the stairs; nothing was what it seemed today.

Tatiana sat up and looked at him expectantly. He shut the door carefully and put the cases down with equal care. He moved easily towards her and kissed her full on the lips. That was what is seems and should be. She kissed him back and then launched into, "What the hell?" Neil put his finger on her lips and said, "Later please." He looked at her, a hard look from head to toe and everywhere in between her full bust, but not too full, lovely little tummy and the curves of her hips, good shapely legs, beautiful smile and long blonde hair. He wanted to feel her soft skin next to his more than he had realised that he wanted anything. At that moment the deaths, the travelling, his worries gave way to that emotion he only felt when he saw her. He loved her, more than any other women, and very differently from his family. He did love her and yet, he had never really told her. He moved to the flight bag and unzipped the front pocket. He pulled out a small package. He handed it to Tatiana and asked her to "Open it please." He stood a little away from her as she pulled at the wrapping paper and the little pink bow. It contained an octagonal box, but she could not see how to open it, no catch, and no clip. She was getting frustrated, she tried to twist it and it did not move. "I can't see it, if I can't open it you big …?" "Look at the top and press the inlaid flower please." She placed her index finger on the inlay and the lid moved; she excitedly pushed it more quickly to reveal a blue velvet cushion with a diamond solitaire. She stood unable to speak, at last she said, "For me?" "I do not intend to marry anyone else, if you say no. So please Tatiana do not say no. Will you marry me?" In that moment there was no game, no going home, and no end of his fieldwork. All there was a pure, sincere and deep feeling of love for one lady, his lady Tatiana. She was in tears. Neil's automatic reaction was that he must have got it wrong and that was why she was crying. It never occurred to him they were tears of happiness. She hugged him and kissed his face, put the ring on and kissed his face all over again. He felt that world was right as they came together in a clinch. Second time today he had thought that to himself. As they held each other, Tatiana moved away for a brief moment to pull the curtains across they were staying in tonight. He heard the hiss of breaking double-glazing and moved to push Tatiana away from the window. Too late, blood was coming out of a neat round hole in her forehead. Now Neil was crying, thinking, but crying as he gently lay his lady down on the floor. He kissed those lips once more and was trying to understand what had happened when the doors burst open. At that moment, he did not care about anything as he launched himself at the first man through the door. His fist met the man's chin in one movement and the man fell with a sickening crack of breaking bone. Neil used the man as a shield against the second man who was trying to pass the first. Two taps rang out and the man, the human shield, had done his job; Neil was alive and fighting for his very existence and revenge of his dead Tatiana. As swiftly as he had chopped the man's hand this morning, he hit the gunman and turned his gun hand on himself. One shot and this man fell to the floor. He could not leave Tatiana; he could not stay. Tears streaming down his cheeks, those cheeks she had been kissing so fervently, he moved to the stairs and looked down, no one. He slowly walked towards the garage door. He stopped and touched a small plastic card in his pocket and the suitcase exploded in the apartment. Tatiana cremated by his hand no one else. No one else on the stairs as he carefully opened the garage door. He stood and surveyed the garage for one brief moment; the doors, of the garage where still locked shut and the Merc was cool as he passed in front of the engine. He continued past the car and pushed a button on the side of the workbench. Another door opened into what looked like another garage. Not so much a garage as a workshop come store of various items like weapons, a motor bike, money, passports and new matching Samsonite luggage. He stepped inside; tears still rolling down his face and pushed the button, which closed the door and put the lights on. *This place is dusty* he thought. It did not matter; nothing mattered until he had sought out and killed those who were behind all of this. Life had now become personal not just the game or even a game, not business. Just personal, intensely personal. In the quietness of this room, he wiped his face and eyes and rang Marianna's phone.

Maurice picked the phone up and answered it. He had been stroking George's brow, when this irritation occurred. "What the hell are you doing answering Mariana's phone Maurice? Where is she?"

Maurice told him of the shoot out and that he was with George now. Neil was angry, something that never happened. He shouted down the phone, "Get out of George's bed or his body and get to the office I will be there in fifteen minutes." He did not wait for a reply. At that, moment as Neil hung up; George's house became a battlefield of bullets and dead bodies. Those of George's himself and then Maurice. There was no time for fancy shooting from Maurice as two hooded men in black had opened fire with Uzi's and another two bodies added to the day's tally of dead men and women. The apartment was a mess. Someone had called the police to come to another shooting. As the police officer from the shooting at the safe house arrived and looked at the dead men. He could not help but smile when he saw it was Maurice's contorted body.

Confusion

Chapter 4

Neil slide down the brick wall in his office. He sat on the floor with his legs out in front of him. He started to cry and broke down in tears, sobbing violently. His feelings for Tatiana were something that he had not realised until she was not there. He could not stop sobbing, his shoulders heaved; he had lost his friend, his companion, his lover and she was to be his wife. He had lost too much; no job was worth this kind of loss. Did his father never really love anyone because he knew it would be like this! How could he describe this loss, the emptiness, the pain in his heart that would not stop or go away? He heard a knock on the door and some clerk came in, looked around and could not see Neil on the floor. He placed a piece of paper on the desk. Neil said, "What is it please?"

"Oh sir, Oh! It is urgent!" Neil put his left hand up, took the piece of paper, and read the following. The neatly typed script said that gunmen, unknown gunmen, at George's house, had shot Maurice and George dead. Shot using Uzi weapons, as cartridges had been found all over the floor. The local police were involved.

Slowly, but with a steady movement, Neil got up from his place on the floor. He stood straight and erect for the second time today he was allowing himself to get angry. Calm quiet anger, the kind that allows a man to rip off someone's head and urinate down the hole to prove they are dead, angry to the point where people were going to pay for the attempted assassination of all the people who were at the safe house today.

Neil straightened his clothes, adjusted his tie, checked his cufflinks had not rolled around and then walked out of the office door and into the director's office without knocking. "May I?" He sat without invitation.

"For Christ's sake Neil will you get out of this country and my area? I cannot afford any more chaos. You are a walking disaster area and you are walking all over my patch. Just go home like you were supposed to!" He was as angry as Neil was, but in his own way. Neil sat still, hands on his knees and waited. The director wiped his brow with a pure white handkerchief, cotton. Shows good taste at least thought Neil. The man rambled on and on about dead staff, London agents, not understanding the situation and then he went quiet.

Neil stood up and walked calmly from the office, shutting the door behind him gently. He walked down the stone steps and came out into the street. It was getting lighter. He smelt bad, had not changed his clothes, and needed a shower. He needed a drink and some breakfast. He turned left at the end of the road and was soon at his favourite café. Was it worth the risk? He opened the door and the little bell rang as the door opened.

"Mr Neil, Mr Neil, and long time you no come to my teashop. You found new tea Shop. You find better teashop. You never find a better teashop than mine! No better tea shops this side of Jianghan plain." Zhou said. "What tea today you want? I think you need Pu er?" Zhou shouted to the waiter behind him and sat down next to Neil. "Something wrong, very wrong, Mr Neil. Tell me now; what can I do for you?" Zhou was dressed in trousers and a loose fitting shirt; he had shoes and socks on, cheap material all over. Zhou was not poor. This was the front for the Chinese Embassy's escape route out of the country and Neil knew he could trust Zhou.

"Things are not good Zhou; do you know?" "Yes I hear and too many people are dead; you no dead Neil!" "Yet," replied Neil quietly and calmly. "May I ask; I need a favour please?" "For you anything, anything Mr. Neil except, money he he, Mr Zhou make joke he he. Where you wanna go Neil, back to China?" Neil knew that Zhou was well informed; should he try for more information? "What do you know about the deaths Zhou?" Neil asked with an even tone almost as if he were ordering tea. The tea arrived and Mr Zhou poured out a bowl of hot tea for Neil and himself. Together they drank tea from plain china bowls and Neil relaxed for a moment.

A man opened the door; the bell rang, and walked in, dressed in black. He was pulling a balaclava over his face. Before Neil could do anything, the waiter had chopped the man's hand and a gun fell to the floor. The man turned and received an old-fashioned upper cut and was out cold. The waiter stood straight and waited for Zhou to say something. "Put him in a chair, tie him up. Oh also take down his trousers and leave them around his ankles. No man can run fast with trousers round ankles."

Neil allowed all this to happen as he continued to drink his tea. Zhou turned to Neil and said "Let's eat; he will take a while before we get information." The waiter finished putting the man on the chair and skilfully tied him up, after dropping his trousers. "Anything in his pockets?" Neil asked, expecting a no as the reply. The waiter felt through the man's pockets, found money, and a piece of paper. Zhou took the money and passed the paper to Neil. At this moment the food arrived, steam buns, seaweed, dumplings, spicy chicken, and steamed vegetables. Neil took more interest in the food, he was hungry, than the piece of paper. Zhou also turned to the food, but counted the money first. "Your value is going up" he turned to Neil and showed him the notes. "Nice to know," said Neil through a mouthful of steam bun. Neil turned the paper towards him as he carried on eating. A slim, attractive and well-shaped woman moved towards Neil and Mr Zhou. "You no come visit me Neil, why you no come to me? You find a better girl" Neil looked up from his food, glanced at the paper and then focused upon the girl. "Tingting your hair is a mess, I am a mess and we are busy trying to sort out a mess. I do not have time at present." "Last two times you say you are busy; but, before that we make sex, good sex. Why no more make sex?" Neil was not in the mood for sex, lovemaking or anything except revenge. Zhou told her to go. She left complaining that she had not had sex in ages and no one loved her.

Mr Zhou turned to Neil, and asked, "Where you wanna go Mr. Neil, now?" Neil looked up with a dumpling skewered on his chopsticks. "I need a safe place to sleep, no distractions, and I mean safe Zhou, and I mean no distractions." "You've got it Mr. Neil, what else you need?" "I will tell you after the food and a sleep please" Neil replied. "My man will talk with him and I will tell you when you wake up. He will be alive for you. You have my word Mr. Neil. Use room 5 upstairs and do not worry a man will be outside all the time. You know which one I mean." Mr Zhou spoke and his staff started running around and moving the man into another room; opening a concealed door behind the cash desk. Neil walked through and the door shut behind him softly. He slowly climbed the stairs and turned into room 5. Plain pastel walls, firm bed on a cheap metal frame. It had Egyptian cotton sheets, pillowcases, and a feather duvet. He undressed and lay between the sheets. Unexpectedly, he remembered school and playing the sweeper in "Bugsy Malone." He had started the singing for "We could have been anything that we wanted to be." He could have been anything, a first from, Oxford, Harvard postgraduate and languages. He could have been anything that he wanted to be. He chose intelligence. Why? Then he was asleep.

The Pieces are not fitting

Chapter 5

Sigs 2 read the stream of death reports from the computer in front of his position. "Jesus what has he been doing?" He had spoken aloud and a clerk said, "Who sir?" "Nothing, sorry nothing to worry about, get me a coffee please." He thought to himself that there is a leak. No not so much a leak as a bloody deluge. Who, where, when, why, what, how? 5W'sH seemed a good place to start as any other. No one had heard from Neil since he had left the director's office that was eight hours with no report, no news, and no contact. This was all going from bad to worse. He stood up, his shift had finished 3 hours ago and he was still in work mode, thinking, review the little evidence and doing what he did best; work out what was happening and why. A coffee mug was dutifully placed in front of him and he mumbled a thank you.

He had gone to the safe house, left the safe house, gone to the Russian's, then the office and now the Chinese perhaps. Nearly all of the important players were now dead. Why was Neil the only one left standing? There was no Chinese sigs traffic worth talking about so was he with the Chinese? The Russian signals traffic picked up as soon as Neil had arrived in the consulate, embassy? He could not remember which. Strange, why the Russians first when he had just flown in from China? He picked up a cream telephone and said get me Wuhan station not on clear, please. He replaced the receiver and carried on thinking, trying to fit the pieces together. He knew about the Chinese girl, she was a plant; but. Why did he go to Tatiana's place? They were supposed to meet in London, dinner together with him and his wife. Why? Sigs 2 slurped his coffee, strong, black so that you can stand the spoon up in it. That was real coffee. He slowly got up, walked over to the biscuit tin, and pulled the lid off. No bourbons, he turned and to no one in particular said, "Which tart ate the last of my bourbons." Heads ducked down and there was no reply save a simple, "That's sexist!" He took out a biscuit out of the tin, put the lid back on, and pushed it tightly down. A Jamie dodger, they were good, as long as the jam was fresh, needed a sealed tin for that. He walked back to his desk in this non-descript, grey walled office in the middle of, oops classified material. He sat in his expensive chair with pump-up lumbar support, side supports, and a headrest. He put his head on the rest and stretched. No new information, no call or message, emails; nothing from Neil, nothing from the Russian. Where was that call to Wuhan station? Why no additional communications from the Chinese, were they involved. Who was playing this game? The whole thing was wrong, the bits that should be there were not and the bits that were there should not have been there, and where was Neil. This was no game. It was wholesale murder.

Wuhan station was in the building that housed a hotel and the shopping centre. You could only approach it from one way in a car or walk, he mused. The glass front to the hotel gave it some class in an area where, at night, it became a bustling market that you could not get through. The chemist on the next block was the escape route, and the metal gates only allowed one person through at a time. He had personally ensured that the route worked before Neil went out there. He had come back a different route to the one Neil had opted for. Why had he gone via the Black Sea, when he knew he was seeing Tatiana in London? Why had he changed the route at the last minute, what had happened? No, no ordered to take that route as a "milk run." Where was the call to Wuhan centre? The blue telephone rang and he picked up the receiver, "Wei, Nin Hao" it would be Wuhan Station.

Neil sat up in bed with a start. He shook his head to try to wake up and remembered the military drill instructor barking that the Queen owned them 23 hours and 59 minutes a day, but the first minute of waking up belonged to them. Well that was the first minute. He looked around the room everything was fine. He rolled over, opened the travel Samsonite bag. Took out, what to most people would have been and odd shaped block of plastic, the phone to ring Sigs 2. He slowly proceeded to open pieces, pull a bit out, and push something there and at last pulled at a stubby aerial. He dialled the code and heard "Wei, Nin hao."

"Who the hell do you think you're talking to?"

"Wuhan station?"

"No it's me, your friendly, not dead yet, on his way home colleague."

"Sigs 2 was not prone to expletives, but he answered with, "Jesus Christ Neil, where are you, how are you, what the hell has happened to you?" This flow of words came out faster than he had wanted them to. He had and still was concerned.

"I am fine, just woken up from a good sleep in a real safe house. I am changing the plan and coming back via Paris and I will make all of the arrangements at my end."

Sigs 2 cut across his words, "The top brass are going crazy, I am instructed to inform you to return to London immediately, no via anywhere and stick to the plan."

"Who gave you that instruction please?" Neil asked. "I can't answer that on this line," was the reply.

"Then just make a note and save the information for my return. Bye old boy, take care; hope the weather is good." Neil had gone!

Sigs 2 scratched his head and sat back in the chair. He had caught Neil's inference and was wondering why the plan could not be changed. Something was very wrong. He looked up and shouted, "Where the hell is Wuhan station?"

Madam Lan and other Ladies

Chapter 6

There was a soft knock at the door and Neil turned to see the door opening. He never slept with anything under his pillow except a handkerchief. He sat up in bed and waited as a petite, dark haired woman entered the room with a breakfast tray. The guard outside, Mr Zhou's protection for him, closed the door behind her. The woman was wearing a traditional red long length Cheongsam Chinese dress with the slits both sides and those funny shoes with no heel and lace up straps. He remembered an invite to a dinner where the servers wore traditional dress and the funny shoes with blocks in the middle. To this day, he could never understand how servers could walk in them, even if they were traditional. The woman approached, with head down, but did not falter with the tray. He could smell coffee, fresh, warm rolls and egg fried rice. "You always say, I bring breakfast; but, must get into bed as well. I say this too move over Neil." She placed the tray by the bed on the side table, stood upright and smiled at Neil; then pulled the Cheongsam over her head and stood before him naked. Before Neil could speak her name, she was beside him. "Madam Lan, what a surprise, you are supposed to be in China?

"No bad troubles in China, I come here to safety with Mr Zhou. He tells me you in the safe room, no speakers, no cameras, no VCR, so I bring you breakfast, coffee and me. What order you like? I know about Tatiana, you need me to help you now! You make breakfast with me and I help you feel better." She pushed herself to touch every part of his body with her nakedness, touching his nakedness everywhere. Well that was how it felt to Neil. She gently kissed his lips and ran her hands over his chest slowly fondling his nipples until they became rock hard. Neil tried to protest and then stopped himself, he felt the soft skin and ran his hands down her back to her cute little rear end and pulled her closer to him as he kissed her lips. Madam Lan skilfully moved her hands powerfully and excited him. At the precise moment, she moved her body effortlessly to sit on top of him and rode him. He held her breast and massaged her as she moved; she let out a moan and called his name.

What had seemed like a few minutes lovemaking, sex she called it, had been much longer and the coffee had turned cold. "I make fresh?" "No stay beside me for a few moments longer and they cuddled each other like lost souls needing comfort. Her black hair had fallen over her breasts as she lay beside Neil. They were holding hands. She softly, "Thanked you" to him and was up, dressed and left as quietly as she had arrived.

Neil lay on his back and looked at the ceiling. He heard a knock at the door this time. It was Mr Zhou with fresh coffee and more rice. Neil sat up in bed and pulled the sheets to him. "Zhou I am not even up yet."

Mr Zhou laughed and said, "You have been up and we have work to do!" He poured Neil and himself a bowl of coffee and sat on the edge of the bed. Zhou was also wearing a Cheongsam, but thankfully did not take it off. "Madam Lan, like you a lot Mr. Neil, she a good woman for you now!" Neil did not reply he was looking at the papers Zhou had placed on the tray beside the coffee. It was a transcript of the interrogation of the man from last night. "He belongs to an organization called the Network." "Never heard of it," interjected Neil. "He was Ukraine." Neil noticed the "was" comment. Neil read the page quickly using his speed reading skills. "How do you know he came from Kiev, Zhou?"

"He was not professional, had papers and an identity card on him. That is why we caught him." Neil asked, "Are you sure it was not a set up a plant, dummy papers?" Neil drank the coffee and waved the bowl for more. Zhou dutifully refilled his bowl and then refilled Neil's. "He gave us an address in Kiev and my men have already checked it out. It exists and is not brothel or a flop house Mr. Neil."

"Yes I can see it here. Was it his house, or another one of these dodgy safe houses?"

"We don't yet know," replied Zhou. "You will go there?" Neil replied with a nod of his head and then looked up and said, "But not yet I need to go back over a few things."

"Don't go getting yourself killed after I have saved you and put you back on your feet so to speak." Zhou looked at him as one brother would look at another, affection and caring, not knowing that nothing he said or did would stop Neil doing what was necessary. Zhou stood up and without another word left. Neil noticed the slight shake of his head as he left the room; the guard pulled the door closed as Zhou walked out.

Neil opened the larger of the two Samsonite cases and looked at the clothes. Yes, "Hom" underwear, cotton shirts, cuff links, Marks and Spencer's suit and a handmade suit. The latter he decided he would wear. He showered and shaved and placed the razor back in the leather, black, toilet bag, zipped it up and pressed the button closed to stop the zip opening again. He applied a little of the L'Oréal Vitalift to his jaw line and rubbed the cream in. He dressed and could not find a tie. He tapped the door and asked the guard for a red silk tiger tie. The guard nodded and Neil shut the door again. Handmade shoes for half the price of a London tailors or shoe makers for that, made in Shrewsbury. There was a knock at the door and the guard presented him with a red silk dragon tie. At the very last moment, Neil noticed the glint of a knife blade in the man's hand covered partly by the tie. Neil moved as if to accept the tie and twisted the man's hand violently. The blade fell, yet the man kept coming. Neil chopped him three times on his neck and it seemed to have no effect. He raised his leg crane style and then kicked him in between his legs. As the guard started to react and fall forward, Neil thought something is wrong this is too easy. The man grabbed at Neil and started to squeeze his rib cage tighter and tighter. Neil's eyes were set to burst, he could not breathe and the pain was sharp as he felt the old rib cage wound pop out again. He saw the man's face and poked him in his right eye, very hard. Pulling his fingers back as the man clasped his face and let Neil go. Neil kicked him again in the groin and made for the open door, shouting for Zhou! The knife caught the top of his hand as he used the doorframe to get into the corridor. He saw the dead guard with a red tiger tie, still held in his hand. Neil had been born in the year of the tiger, like his father and that was a give-away with the dragon tie. The man was after him and Neil was not sure where anyone else was in the house or the teashop. "Get to the ground floor" he said to himself and carried on running to the stair well. Neil glanced back and saw the man fall over the dead guard as he was still holding his eye. Running down the stairs Neil held the handrail firmly, now was not the time to fall. He reached the ground floor and heard the man on the stairs. Neil frantically looked about for Zhou, where was he. Neil found him, throat cut on the floor as he fell over him. Neil rolled to his left and saw the man reaching the bottom of the stairs. He looked at Zhou again and still tightly holding a gun in his hand. Neil picked up the dead hand and did not try to take the gun, he held the hand and pointed it at the fake guard and pushed Zhou's fingers on the trigger of a Glock 17. He did not stop to ask the question of himself how Zhou had managed to get his hands on one of these. The man moved his hand from his eye to his chest and fell forward crashing into a chair. The smell told Neil that the man was no more a threat. The mess was profound and it looked like the remains of a battlefield. It struck Neil that everywhere he went they killed people. He could not understand who or why? Neil put a chair upright and sat down. He surveyed the scene before him and wondered if the police would arrive eventually. Broken furniture, dead bodies, blood and excrement causing a rotten smell of death to his nostrils. His thoughts moved to Madame Lan, was she safe, had she escaped. She had said she had come here for safety, some safety. This was becoming a game of last man or woman standing. A game he needed to win. He collected his things from the safe room and left the teashop before the police arrived.

He took a cab to the first safe house, where all the problems had started. He stopped the cab at the top of the road and walked with the cases down to the metal doors. Neil looked up and down the street and then pressed the code, which opened the small door. He walked into the courtyard and moved to open the door that he had opened only 24 hours before. This time he saw the curtain move in the next apartment's window. A glimpse of a woman looking at him and then she was gone. Neil opened the door, went in and shut it firmly behind himself. He placed the cases in the bedroom to his left and walked into the kitchen. He poured himself a soft drink and went to the window by the door. At that, moment there was a small rap. He opened the door and to his surprise, the woman next door was standing there. "Hello my name is Irina, I live next door. Well I have done for the last

6 months. I put the flowers out." She pointed to the hanging baskets. "Would you like to come in for a drink or something?" Neil asked. "I don't want to disturb you; you must have been travelling, cases and things." Neil looked at this woman, forty if that, and his height, straight skirt and a tight top, which showed her shape and the curves of her body. Neil stood back and let her come into the safe house. It was against departmental rules, but he did not care anymore. The apartment did not have a lounge; a bedroom with a television and a kitchen with a toilet built in. He showed her into the room with the double bed and the TV. She sat down on the edge of the bed and with big blue eyes looked up at him, examining him closely. This was not a come on; it was inspecting someone she had seen before. Yet he did not know her. He would have remembered the eyes and the fair coloured hair, the shape of the body and the fact that when she had stood at the door she was not as tall as he was. She smoothed out her skirt, nervousness Neil thought. "Would you like a coffee or a drink of something else? "Something soft and cold if possible please," she answered. Neil walked into the kitchen, took out a couple of sodas from the fridge, picked up to Coca Cola glasses, and walked back. The woman was now sitting on the bed with her legs up, with no attempt to hide the sun-tanned expanse of flesh. A come on Neil thought and put the glasses down and poured the sodas slowly. He felt tired, even though he had slept at Mr Zhou's place. Needing information, this seemed like a good idea, at the time. Now he was not so sure. She was very confident and very beautiful Neil thought as he handed her the glass. Dam he had forgotten the ice. "Sorry do you want ice, the drinks came from the fridge?" "No this will be wonderful. Please sit here" She patted the place where she had first sat down and Neil obliged as she moved her legs away from him. "So what do you do besides the flowers?" Neil asked. He was lousy at small talk and he knew it. Seduction was a

different matter, but small talk, no! "Me" she said in a manner of fact way, "I am an accountant for a local firm." The TV suddenly burst into the Scorpions Winds of Change. "I love this song," she said. Neil turned down the volume from the remote, which was closer to him. He found the words of Roxette's "It must have been love" came into his mind and he thought of apartment's, dead bodies and people he would never see again. Somewhere in the distance, he heard "Are you alright?" Neil realised that a single tear was coming down his cheek and the woman leant forward and brushed it away. Her skin was soft and her touch gentle as he pulled a white handkerchief from his trouser pocket. "Sorry, bad 24 hours" he replied, used it to wipe his face, and then folded the material, and placed it back into his pocket. What was the matter with him? He looked at the woman who seemed very intent on understanding why he was the way he was. Neil shook himself and inadvertently said out loud, "Someone has walked over my grave" "I hope not," said the fair-haired woman. "Irina" he said, "Have you eaten yet? There is a little place just up in the square that does the oddest wraps, but they taste great. Would you like to join me?"

They started strolling up to the square a few moments' walk away. Irina slipped her hand into his and squeezed it gently. "Things will get better," she said to him. Neil did not remove her hand or take his away as they walked in the bright sunlight up the street to the top of the hill and turned right. This was the main road with trolley buses and went straight into the square. They crossed the road and avoided the mass of traffic, but she still held his hand in hers. Neil stood in front of the stand and ordered two wraps, explaining carefully to the young man inside the stall that he did not want cucumber or pickle and no sauce. Irina explained that he should go heavy on the spicy sauce, but light on the chips inside the wrap please.

They sat on a wooden bench and ate the hot wraps. They tasted good and suddenly the world seemed a brighter place to Neil. Irina got sauce dripping on her napkin and Neil gave her his to mop up. Neil turned to Irina and said, "OK, you're an accountant and you have the apartment next to mine, what do you do in your spare time?" "Oh me? Well I sit and listen to the man next door and have watched him cry. I tease and watch people." That was the opening he needed. "You were there yesterday weren't you? He asked her. "Yes" she said, "I saw the man come at you and you shot the little man. I shut the shutters and did not look anymore when the people and then the police came. I am an accountant, what are you?" "A linguist, professional administrator and …" he tailed off. "Someone or some people are trying to kill you, why?" she said quickly. Irina was sitting close to him and he could feel her body heat. Neil sat up straight and said, I am trying to get home." "I am just trying to get home Irina." He had repeated himself. Neil was shocked and indecision filled his face. Was he losing it? Is this why the mandarins had said he should stop fieldwork? Had this happened to his father? Did his father die as people were trying to kill him? Did his father just walk away from the game? His father, David, had never called it wrong in many years. Neil knew, from his mother's comments that it had played on his mind. What if Neil was calling it wrong and that was why so many people were dead! Enough people had died already. Was it his wrong call? Was he now calling the game incorrectly for the first time, ever? Irina took his hand and said, "Let's get some drinks and go back to my place." Neil could not help himself as he replied, "Are you leading me astray?" "That depends upon what you mean by astray," she laughed. As they got up from the bench, Neil placed his hand in hers and she did not draw back. They walked closely, but in silence back the way they had come. Soon at the metal door, Neil tensed and she felt it in his hand. "I will go first and you come to my apartment not yours." "OK," he replied. She had left the smaller metal entrance open and Neil could see no one in the courtyard. He shut the metal door quietly and walked to the bottom of the wooden stairs, which were close to Irina's front door. He would check everything later. The yard had been cleaned, but by whom? Was it his people, the Russian, or the Network? Irina called for him to come into her apartment, which was the mirror of his unsafe "safe" house. She had put you up bed that doubled as a sofa. "Sit down," she said as he came through the doorway. "I really must check a few things first before I can accept your hospitality please. I just need to check around outside, if you don't mind." "I can help, or perhaps watch," she said brightly. The appeal was genuine and Neil found himself responding with a, "Yes OK, but don't touch anything please." Neil walked back through the open front door and Irina following behind him. He noticed the variety of high heel shoes of various colours. That did not seem to be an accountant's weakness. Just like a woman, he thought. He then turned his attention to the bottom of the wooden stairs. He ran his hand along the seasoned wood of the staircase and was thinking about the girl being a setup. As he moved his hand slowly, he felt a break where no break should be. He looked hard and could just make out a crack in the wood. A crack that should not have been there. Unless, he pushed hard and pulled, nothing happened, at that moment Irina placed her hand on the side of the Newell post, Neil heard a click. A small door flicked open. "Opps sorry, was that me?" she asked. "I didn't mean to, I was just ..." Neil cut across her and said, "Don't worry and thank you anyway." A small doorway had opened. That is why the second man was a dwarf. He looked inside and saw pieces of food, cigarettes butts, a ripped small jacket, box of rounds unused, and a greasy fingerprint on the lid of the box. Neil carefully put the box in a plastic bag he found lying around. Looked at the jacket. All the labels were ripped out. There was no way of knowing if it was local or from anywhere else. Neil backed out and was about to say something when he noticed the stray cat again. The cat rubbed up against his leg and then wandered into the cupboard, for it was too small to be a room. The cat disappeared and then reappeared further down the stair well. Back entrance he thought and went to investigate. This opening was far too small for any normal sized man and too big for the cat not to be interested. The cat's fur was up and he would not move. Neil decided that he would not venture further into the gap. The cat did not move as it was staring into the hole again. Neil looked for a broom and saw one behind Irina leaning against the wall. Irina had not moved since the Newell post incident. Picking it up he thrust it into the hole. The broom handle was shattered into two pieces as a metal slab fell down and blocked the hole completely. That would have been his head. Nevertheless, it was not meant to him he thought. A safety measure or protection. He tapped the box in the plastic bag and said to Irina, "How about that drink please." Irina went into the apartment and this time Neil followed closely behind her. He put the box on the hall table. "What's so special about the box?" Irina asked him as she poured the drinks. She had poured two large whiskeys, without asking him if that was what he wanted. How did she know he liked whiskey? Neil answered as if nothing was out of place, "I should be able to get some sort of print from the box. That way I can find out who the dwarf was." "Oh! Don't call people that please," she said with a pained expression. "Why not?" asked Neil. "I really think that it is a dreadful term to use to describe people." "Oh I understand what you mean," said Neil. "Do you, do you really?" she asked. "Yes I fell out with an official once for not allowing him to use the term ethnic minorities. Whatever happened to communities? I was born in King's Lynn, in England and they had communities. My dad had communities in London, not ethnic minorities." Why had he mentioned his father? Irina had resumed the position on the sofa that she had adopted before they went to investigate. Neil sat beside her legs and took out his mobile. He clicked a button on the side, took a picture and then pressed the send button. Moments later, he knew that the people in London would check to see if they could find a match from someone, they knew.

He took a gulp pf his drink as he looked up. Irina was fast asleep, head on one side similar to the way he slept. He got up slowly, took the cover, and placed it over her. He carefully tucked her in and left closing the door quietly. He suddenly felt tired, still checking to see no one was about. Why had he left? He was not sure, something about the woman was special, but! He did not want to impose. He walked the few paces back to the unsafe, safe house. He closed that door quietly so as not to wake anyone. He walked into the kitchen and took out his laptop from the travel bag. He felt hungry. He stopped and moved to the door. Also checking to see if the window next to the door was closed. Both were and he was safe. He opened the cupboards and found some cut, fresh bread and cold meat in the refrigerator, ham. Ham was not his favourite. He preferred corned beef. Putting two slices of meat in between slices of bread, he poured himself a glass of milk and sat down at the laptop. A circular icon flashed up on the screen, so he clicked on it. The screen suddenly filled with the face of his friend Sigs 2. The voice said, "I've seen you look better you old fart." Neil promptly replied, "Not so much of the old; it is too near the truth. How are you?" Sigs 2 ignored his comments and started talking at a rapid pace. He started into, "Anymore dead bodies in the last thirty minutes? You're still alive." Neil asked, "Was the print of anyone we know? "Yes a small time hood from Kyiv actually. Does that Help? Petty theft, running errands for others got him noticed by us." Neil replied, "A name and an address might a little more." "I'll send what we have, not in clear, OK?" "Is that the best you can do? Neil said absentmindedly, in an instant he changed he had changed he had heard something outside. "I have to go, something's come up." "A woman I guess you old rascal." The line went dead and Neil shut the laptop lid down and moved to the door.

He could noises outside, a muffled girl's cry. He opened the door gingerly to find Irina, trying not to be dragged out of her front door by a six-foot man with shoulders to match. Neil walked out as if nothing was happening; yet as the man turned to look at him, still holding Irina tightly, he felt the full force of a chop to the bridge of his nose. Quickly followed by a knee into his groin and another chop to the side of his head. He slowly released Irina, as he seemed to form a puddle on the floor as he sank into the ground. Irina was shaking uncontrollably and tears had ruined her make up. Neil put his arm around her and gently guided her into his apartment. She went in and Neil closed the door He tuned to look at the puddle on the floor. He was out cold. Neil thought to himself, "Military training does pay off sometimes." Nevertheless, Neil did love to hate the Physical Training Instructor. What was her name? Margaret, no, Maggie. A big woman, strong and powerful enough to teach men unarmed combat. Not a blemish on her skin and she was fit!

Turning his mind back to the job at hand. He rolled the man over and checked his pockets. No wallet or pocket book, some car keys with an old Ford key fob. What looked like a door key, a funny shaped key, which looked as if half had been broken, a pistol a Fort 12 Ukrainian Police weapon? This plaything had a presentation finish. No warrant card or something that might give him a clue who this man was. The man moaned and started to get to his feet, very unsteady and very slowly. He found himself starring into his own gun barrel. He looked up at Neil's eyes with pure contempt and hate. He said in Broken English, "This is a private affair, stay out of it English, if you know what is good for you!" Neil jerked the gun barrel up to tell the man to stand up fully. As he got up straight Neil pushed him onto the back wall of the courtyard. The man involuntarily went to put his hand up to his neck; but Neil rested the gun barrel on his arm and he stopped. Dangerous move if the man had been any good, but he was not. Neil patted him down and found a pair of handcuffs on his leather belt. He unclipped the cuffs and put them on man, very carefully. He could sense Irina's eyes on him looking through the closed, but not shuttered, window. "Кто вы мудак? Who are you asshole? Neil asked him in Russian. The man seemed to relax a little and replied, "Я здесь по делу с дамой так Отвали англичанина, инспектор Shapko." (I am here on official business with this woman so sod off Englishman, Inspector Shapko.) Neil kicked him again and he buckled forward moaning and swearing in Ukraine. Neil switched to perfect Ukraine and said, "На жаль про це, але я не хочу бути розповів Відвали на будь-якій мові. Почнемо знову, як ви сказали мені, що це особиста справа, і тепер він є офіційним бізнес. Я думаю, що ви лежав ублюдок Shapko". ("Sorry about that but I hate being told to sod off in any language. Let us start again as you told me this was private affair and now it is official business. I think you are a lying bastard Shapko.") Neil dragged him back up and the so-called inspector rolled over and sat with his back to the wall. Both his hands were lovingly cupped around his scrotum. "Таким чином, ви скажіть мені, що це приватне, офіційний бізнес тоді?" ("So tell me what this private, official business is then?") Neil asked as he took a pace backwards in case the man tried anything. ""Кто, черт возьми, ты ублюдок?" ("Who the hell are you bastard?") "Майор Нил Олаф, специальный раздел

5, и вы?" ("Major Neil Olaf, special section 5 and you?") At that, the so-called inspector tried to straight himself up. He could not he was too sore and in too much pain. Sharp cutting pain that meant Neil had done some damage. "Мне очень жаль, сэр … Я не знаю, что она была связана с раздела Мне так жаль, я просто думал, что я мог бы получить … Она используется для включения трюки для меня Ну, я думал, что это было то же самое девочка. Я должен ошибаться." ("I am so sorry sir; I didn't know she was associated with your section. I am so sorry. I just thought I could get … She used to turn tricks for me. Well I thought it was the same girl. I must be mistaken.") Neil pulled him up to his feet and then moved closer to his face, gun still in his hand. Softly, menacingly, but quietly so only the man could hear, "Если я вижу или слышу, что вы были в 50 метрах от этой дамы, я убью тебя! Все ясно здесь? "Да." "Кристально чистый инспектор?" "Да, да!" ("If I see or hear that you have been within 50 metres of this lady I will kill you! Are we clear here? "Yes." "Crystal clear Inspector?" "Yes, yes!") The Inspector, if that is what he really was, had started to move towards the metal doors, unsteady and not able to walk quickly. He did not look back.

Neil walked back into the apartment and found Irina the other side of the door, clutching a pillow and tears running down her cheeks.

Holiday to Kyiv

Chapter 7

She went to sleep in his bed and what could have been a great love scene became a quiet moment. He covered her with a blanket and went to the kitchen to leave her to sleep. He checked the computer and found the name of details of the dwarf and he had the address from the teashop. He sat back and put the chair on two legs as he thought and reflected upon the trip from Wuhan. He thought about his father. This was the road he had travelled and never got home. No body, no message, no nothing. Was history repeating itself? Was this supposed to be his last journey? This was not so much the game as chaos in death alley. Would he never get home like his father?

His mind switched to something that Sigs had said, in terms of sticking to the plan. If he could mis quote his father's idol John Wayne, "The hell I am." Neil thought back to the situation where he killed was one of his own men. He had fired the shot. He had called the retreat from the hail of bullets and then someone ran into his zone of fire. Chaos all around, Neil lifted his weapon and shot the man dead. One round; it took only one round. It was only as the man fell that Neil realised that it was one of his squad. He knew that if he went back the way the squad had arrived they could expect more firefights and more killings. Neil gathered the remaining men and went back on a different route. Through Aozoua village and another fire fight. Bodies fell like leaves from an autumnal tree as they drove through them killing everyone as they went. It was after that action that he stopped using a gun and used his wits instead. They had finished the day making earl grey tea in the field hut of their camp. That jolted Neil back to reality. Tea he thought I could drink a cup of tea, Earl Grey but real tea; some "lu cha" (green tea). He looked at all of the details and then rang the Russian consulate, spoke to Eric and ordered another Russian passport in the name of Irina Olaf, his wife. Neil passed her name and a made up date of birth, which was too close to the truth to be anything but coincidence. December 19 1974. He put his phone down and went back to thinking about what was really happening. He absentmindedly dialled the office and spoke to the "on-duty" controller. "Oh! It is you. Oh well. I will need two first class tickets to Kyiv in the morning please." The reply was a quizzical, "Two Sir?" "Yes two and tell the station controller to meet me at the bar inside the airport. It will be coffee for three." "But you said tickets for two Sir?" "Idiot the controller is not coming with me. Tickets for two, coffee for three; go it?" Neil did not hear the mumbled as he put down the phone again. He drank his now cold green tea and felt tired. It was getting late. He threw a switch and watched the shutters come down over all of the windows and the outside door. He thought that he heard the outer click of the escape exit. However, it did not matter he and Irina were safe.

He walked into the bedroom. He got carefully into bed with his back to her semi naked body. She pushed into him and her bra catch caught his back. He moved away a little. She followed him and the catch caught him again. He said in a low voice, "If you want to be that close the bra comes off." She sleepily replied, "Please undo me." Neil undid the catch and she took the bra of and let it fall to the floor. She then pushed back into him and pulled him around to cuddle her. She was cold and he cuddled her to get her warm, feeling her soft skin touching his. Lovemaking was out of the question sleep was needed and this was gentle and relaxing. She warmed up quickly and pushed into his middle with her cute rear end. He listened to her breathing as it became regular and slow. The he fell asleep for his regular four hours.

Neil was awake when Irina rolled over and placed her arm across his chest. Her beasts touched his side and she snuggled into him again. This was OK for a few more moments. Nevertheless, he would make breakfast and wake her up. They needed to be on the move. He gently slide from the bed and walked back to the kitchen. He looked at himself as he passed the mirror that was the escape exit really. Showing signs of age, he thought. Nevertheless, his legs were still in good shape for a man his age. However, the scars and marks of his job were always present. He looked at the mark on his knee and remembered the neck flip that saved his life, but caused him to put his teeth into his own kneecap. Some luck escape, he thought to himself. Neil clicked the door and checked that no one was the other side of the mirror, in the kitchen, looking in. "Old habits die-hard."

Having prepared a light breakfast of scrambled eggs on toast, fresh juice and coffee he took a tray into the bedroom, put it on the floor and kissed Irina's cheek. What had the inspector meant about her? Another problem or riddle to solve thought Neil. "Was she an ex-hooker?" She stretched and brought the covers up over her breasts. "Breakfast" he said, "We have to catch a plane." "What do you mean a plane to catch?" she asked. As she leant forward to take the tray, the bedclothes fell away and exposed her beautiful body to Neil. This was really the first time in light, so that he could see her nakedness. Irina did not flinch or move the clothes back. She used the spoon to put an egg on her toast and munched happily. Neil poured the coffee and took a long hard drink of espresso. Irina did not seem to mind that her body was exposed and she could see Neil looking at her. Neil was looking into her eyes not at her chest. She put pillows behind her and sat upright. One leg came out of the covers and the other remained under so that her lower half was not fully visible. Neil noticed this; but did not comment. "So where are we going? Why should I come with you? Do I owe you something?" Irina asked. Neil's reply was matter of fact, "That man, who you did not explain will be back when his gonads are not so sore. I have to go up to Kyiv and I feel it would be safer for you and me if we went as a couple. Oh, we are a married couple your new name is Irina Olaf. OK?" "Why" was the firm reply? "Because, he paused, I want to keep you safe. You are the only person in the last twenty four hours who has not died on me." "But what will I wear?" "We can sort that out in Kyiv, you can shop can't you? I will pay." "Why do I have to be your wife? Did we do it last night? If so it must have been "devastating" as I don't remember a thing"? "No we slept, we did nothing except sleep Irina." "Oh! Jesus why not? What is wrong with me?" She threw the bedclothes from her body exposing herself fully to Neil. He sighed and said to himself, "A man can never be right in a woman's eyes. Damned for making love; damned for not making love" Still there was not time for this. "Aren't you going to answer me?" Irina called as he walked into the kitchen to take a shower. He had his back to the shower door when he heard it open and felt her hands washing his back. "Don't you find me the least bit attractive?" She moved her hands towards his lower regions. "Yes I do, and no we don't have time now!" Neil turned and returned the compliment by soaping her gently. He then rinsed himself and got out, whilst Irina finished showering.

They were in the bedroom dressing like an established couple not looking at each other, yet seeing what the other was doing. When they were dressed, Irina said, "I don't have my bag, or phone. I'll just nip next door and I need to change these things." "No that would not be a good idea" Neil replied too quickly to be calm. He reached into his travel bag and pulled out a mobile and some money. "Take these, use these please." He handed them to her, stopped in front of her and gave her the items he had been holding. It was then he gently pulled her waist towards him and kissed her full on the lips. Not a hard, aggressive kiss, but a lingering, gentle, strong embrace. He stopped and went to move back; but she moved forward and kissed him with the same force and meaning. He liked the taste of this woman. He stood back and really looked at her, hard and long. She was stunning and he meant stunning! A detailed long look that would mean he could remember her anywhere, anytime. Her face was relaxed and line free, beautiful blue eyes, blonde, silky hair, a perfect shape, and curves where there should be curves. She was a few centimetres shorter than he was. Enrapt by her beauty, she broke his silence with the comment "I simply won't go anywhere in these clothes." Neil sighed, he knew the feeling, "OK but don't be surprised at what happens next, please follow me." They walked into the kitchen and Neil pushed the button at the side of the mirror. It opened and he stepped aside to let Irina go first. Irina dutifully went through the mirror. He walked in behind her crossing the small room and pushed what looked like a doorbell. He ignored the video recording equipment. Irina started to speak and then stopped herself. The doorbell opened a slightly smaller door and they were standing in Irina's lounge. "Please Irina be very quick, just throw a few things in a bag or just change. We can buy whatever you need in Kyiv." "How the …" Neil cut her off" you should never have been allowed to rent this place; it is part of the escape route for our safe house. Be quick please love." Was that the Londoner in him or was he falling for this woman? She did as he had asked and changed clothes into black pants and a figure-hugging top. There was no attempt to hide or turn away she just changed her clothes. Neil went back through, picked up his matching, Samsonite luggage, and then joined Irina in her lounge. "Why do we need those?" she asked, "You will see in good time, please follow me and stay close Irina." He moved over to the panel beside the front door. When he had visited last night, he scanned to see if everything was in its place. She had not changed anything, just put up the flowers outside. He punched in a series of numbers and the door keypad, which he had opened by pulling back a small wooden panel. He looked at the small screen and checked that the door in the courtyard was open. It was; he pulled Irina to him. "Darling this is sudden, we don't have time" was all she could say before a lift started to take them down to the underground garage. She sensed that if he had not pulled her to him the sides of the lift might well have caught her. It was a squeeze, the two of them and two bags. The lift stopped silently and Neil let her go saying, "Sorry." "Not on account of me," she said, "I liked being." Neil turned and kissed her lips and gave her a gentle squeeze. She blushed and smiled at him. They were in an empty garage with a set of steps and a car lift. Neil led the way up the steps and the opened a door into the street at the end of the road, near to the corner, and saw a black car was waiting for them.

Neil said in Russian "Благодарю вас, выйти и идти обратно ключи будут на столе в аэропорту приблизительно 45 минут." ("Thank you, get out and walk back the keys will be at the desk in the airport in about 45 minutes.") The man got out and Neil put the bags on the back seat and opened the door for Irina. He drove down streets as if he knew them, which he did arriving at the airport in good time. He opened the door for Irina;

she was not used to this kind of treatment. She put her knees together, sliding her legs out of the car, and stood up. Neil closed the door, then collected the luggage, and locked the door as they walked to the entrance. He had already cased the parking lot as he had opened the car door and went around letting Irina out. No one about, yet! They walked into the airport entrance and turned right towards the offices and ticket counters. Neil knocked on a non-descript door with no sign or notices. After some time a small bespectacled man opened the door. He was tutting to himself and Neil opened the door wider for Irina to enter. "Take the keys please Jack. Are the passport here?" "Tut, yes tut, they are good ones as well, tut." "Your nerves are getting worst Jack," Neil spoke to him as an older man would speak to a younger, although Jack was much older than Neil was. "Are you ready to take us through please?" "Tut, yes this way please, tut, the lady follow me first, tut, you know the way Neil, tut. Please do not look at anyone as we go through, tut, please, tut, tut, tut!" Irina was trying not to have her mouth fall open with shock. They walked through offices and seemed to moving around the building this way. Jack tutting all the way and eventually he opened a door and they were in the departure lounge. Neil moved past Irina and went over to an older man sitting in the bar area. The man was reading a newspaper, but it was upside down. As Neil approached, he moved the paper the right way up and looked up and around the near empty lounge. "You're late, as usual. Where are you going to cause chaos now?" he asked as Irina and Jack joined them. "We are off the Kyiv, have you go the tickets?" Neil was less than pleased at the man's tone of voice; but did not repeat the harshness in his reply. "You are not sticking to the plan at all." "Have you got the tickets please? I hope you brought replenishment as usual?" "The money is in the bag here" and the man threw a small black pouch towards Neil. "Twice the amount; but, you will have to explain why there are two of you to London central. Why are you not sticking to the plan? Sigs 2 sent a message, here it is! It says, Stick to the plan as the boat leaves in two hours." Neil screwed up the note and put it in his pocket. He turned to face the section head and said in a low and very menacing voice, "This route killed my father. I am not going to let it to kill me. My game, my rules, my life, any questions?" There was a brief pause and everyone in the group looked at Neil, who picked up his travel bag and grasped Irina's hand. They walked through to the loading lounge and sat with his back to a wall.

After a few moments, Irina looked at him and gave him a brief smile. He was quiet. Neil only got this quiet when he was angry. However, Irina would never know what was normal for him, as he simply did not tell her? He did not say anything. Neil closed his eyes and tried to remember what his father looked like, before his mother had taken him away. He could not. He thought that he had seen his father on an underground train when he was 21 years old. The man he had seen was every bit an executive in appearance, but also a "grey man." There was something else about him. Neil had glared at the man for about five stops before he got off and disappeared in the crowd. Neil really meant disappeared! He was not in the queue to get into the way out. There were no other exits to the next platform or another line. He was not on the platform at all. He had disappeared before his very eyes.

This last home run was becoming an absolute crapshoot and the crap was falling on him. It seemed to be the prisoner dilemma game all over again. Was he the potential prisoner? He opened his eyes and saw that Irina was worried, wrinkled brow. "Sorry love for that outburst" he had done it again, was it his Londoner background or …?

They boarded the plane together and sat in the two first class seats. Neil asked Irina to sit by the window, which she did. He sat on the aisle seat and carefully checked out the other first class passengers. The man in the non-descript suit in row three was as tall as Neil thought at which point his mobile rang and he looked at the number and switched it off. He suddenly started to laugh as he saw the flight attendant bringing drinks. "What" asked Irina? "Nothing just remembering the Joan Collins and Leonard Rossitor advert for Cinzano." "Oh!" she said, "the one where he tips the drink down her cleavage? Don't even think of it!" Neil laughed and took Irina's hand in his. She smiled and settled herself into the seat for take-off. At that moment, the flight attendant said to a man that the toilets were at the back of the plane. He should use those. The man raised his voice and pushed past her. He was at Neil's elbow when he dropped a piece of paper into Neil's lap and turned, apologised and went back through the partition and curtained doorway. Neil looked at the piece of paper as if someone had just dropped a pile of dung in his lap. Looking up, but not touching the folded paper, Neil wondered, "Had the man left the note or was it from the man across the aisle." The aircraft was taxing out to take off and the flight attendant asked was he, "Alright?" Neil replied that he was and she sat down and strapped herself in for take-off. Only then did he seem to acknowledge the piece of paper. Irina was about to touch it when Neil said, "No!" He pulled her hand back and let go of her other. He took a pen from his pocket and carefully put it in between the folds so that he could lift the paper on the armrest. He moved closer to Irina and further way from the piece of paper. The plane was banking to the left to go north, so he waited before he did anything next. The man opposite him in the aisle asked, "Aren't you going to look at it?" Neil replied, "If you are so keen you look at it." The man leant across the aisle and touched the paper, which flared and burnt his fingers. He dropped the paper and Neil stamped on it to put it out. "How did you know Irina whispered in his ear?" "I didn't!" replied Neil. The flight attendant heard the man's cry and unbuckled her belt to see what the matter was. By the time she had reached him, the man had stopped breathing. There was a fuss and people coming and going, until the crew decided that he had suffered a heart attack and the cry was when he had felt the pain. They covered him over with a blanket. The flight continued its direction north and towards Kyiv. Neil sat in silently in thought, slowly rubbing his shoe sole on the carpet of the aircraft compartment. This was his way of easing stress. As the plane started to go for its approach Irina pushed her hand into his and whispered in his ear, "I thought you said I would be safer with you?" Neil instinctively replied, "We are not dead yet!" Neil's mind was racing ahead to the landing. How was he to ensure that they collected their luggage without attracting attention? A tannoy message told the passengers that they would be disembarking the plane from the rear doors. Neil called the flight attendant over and explained that they would disembark from the front. He pulled out an official looking pass and the attendant acknowledged his request telling another flight attendant to open the front doors as soon as the plane had come to a standstill. Neil and Irina walked down the empty gangway before the police and first aid officials arrived to look at the body. The tall man was ushered off the plane at the rear door and his protestations were to no avail. The police could deal with him later.

Irina asked, "What was the pass; how did you arrange this?" Neil was in work mode, he did not answer. Checking everything around them as they walked into the terminal building. A uniformed official saluted Neil and asked them to follow him. No customs check at the national airport and no collection of luggage. They were already waiting for them in an office with a view of the bus stops outside the terminal building. Neil was waiting for a car. However, at the last minute he said, "Thank you, we will take the coach. Much to Irina's surprise." "Why the coach? What is wrong with a taxi? I don't want to go on a coach with lots of people." "Safety in numbers," Neil laughed as the man opened a door and escorted them to the bus stop. Neil would have been happier without the escort. This time he sat by the window and Irina said nothing. She thought to herself, that *she was not happy. She looked lost and did not understand. Why had she allow herself to go with him? Is he married, no ring? Where are we going now and why are we going on a bus after the incident on the plane. Why did he not make love to me? Is he a homosexual? Oh, my god what have I got myself into now; all this because I did not pay the rent and stole a few things from the apartment to pawn.* She knew how she was in this mess. The Network had ordered her. Neil did not know this small but simple fact. The driver finished collecting the money for the tickets and the bus pulled off towards the international terminal. She noticed that Neil's eyes were everywhere as they pulled up at the stop outside the terminal. There were very few seats left and only three people managed to get on. Neil watched them take their seats as the coach pulled up the road, parked to allow the driver to get the money from the new passengers. The new people were sitting at the back of the coach. Once the driver had taken the money and sat back down, it began its forty-minute journey to Kyiv train station.

    Neil sat, lost in thought, wondering if this is what had happened to his father on his last home run. His mind turned to the address in his pocket. He needed to find its location in the city. He could not guess what he might encounter when he did find it. The journey was uneventful thank heavens. Workers, dressed in shabby work clothes got on or off at various stops before they arrived in the city and the bus worked its way to the station. Neil took the luggage from the compartment under the coach and noticed that there was a red sticker on his luggage. He quickly pulled them off and left it in the compartment. Irina and he moved away from the coach. He selected a "real" taxi not the overcharging touts. They got in and Neil asked for the Olympic. He looked back at the bus and noticed a group of people had gathered around it, as something was wrong. He did not care to find out what. They arrived at the hotel in a few minutes and Neil led them through the downstairs approach located on floor one. He pushed the lift button for floor two. There was no sign to say reception or anything; but he knew where he was going. Irina just looked at him in total amazement. The receptionist took his papers and said, "Your room is ready and is on the top floor." Handing him a white plastic key and asked him in perfect English, "Is there anything else needed?" Neil shook his head and moved around the corner to the lift. The lift was not large but allowed them and the luggage the two matching suitcases to be comfortable as they ascended the two remaining floors to their room. Neil opened the door and let Irina in first. It was a pleasant room pastel blue in colour, nicely furnished with a double bed, writing table and TV. She turned to him and said, "Ok where are you sleeping?" Neil replied, "As a matter of fact on the floor." He closed the door and locked it. Noticing a peephole in the door, Neil opened the toilet door so that it now completely stopped the main door from opening. "Expecting more trouble?" "Not yet," he replied and put the cases on the side table by the desk. "Use the phone and this credit card to buy some clothes please. I will take you to dinner tonight. A nice restaurant down town. I have no problem with you buying expensive clothes, but please not showy. Try something classic." Irina took the card and started to say, "Why can't I" then stopped herself. Instead, she asked, "Are you going out?" "Yes and please don't open the door to anyone. I will knock twice and then a third time before you open the door and let me in," he said. Neil then rummaged in his suitcase and took out an old coat and a Canon rebel camera. He quickly changed his clothes and looked for the world as if he was a tourist on holiday. Camera around his neck he turned and leant forward to Irina. "Darling I know this is not the best, but please trust me" He went to kiss her and she moved away from him. So he turned, opened the door, and left.

 Neil descended in the lift to the first floor, left the hotel the way he had entered it. The rain had started, and he did not have an overcoat. He cut past the other hotels using them for cover and descended the hill through the park. Not many people about and he stopped to check that no one was following him or had suddenly stopped walking in front. The space behind him was an open parking lot and no cover. Anyone could be standing still in the rain. No one was there. He walked on down, thinking to himself that if he had to run down these steps he would probably break his ankle, they were old, steep, and irregular. He made his way past the closed conference centre, and carried on, towards the Olympic stadium the home of Dynamo Kyiv football club. At the corner of the stadium entrance and the entrance road stood a man sheltering from the rain near the turnstiles. Neil checked his pace and slowed to look around. The posters for Scorpion and other pop groups were fading, no cars on the entrance area and no coaches. Only a tram rattled past on the main road as it turned away from him to continue its journey, packed with people keeping out of the rain. Neil walked up to the man an asked for a light, and then asked for a cigarette. The man produced both, looked at him and said, "You should have followed the plan Neil." "Yes you old fart, and I could have been killed too." Sigs 2 did not like fieldwork and disliked being out of London. The two men walked up towards the metro entrance and Neil said, "There is a great little food stall here, hungry?" "Does it sell beer as well? There is one hell of a stink about you and you have picked up some woman? Now please in simple terms tell me what is going on and why I have had to give up a perfectly good office to arrive in Kiev and get soaked waiting for you?

Neil order two chicken wraps and told the young man no sauces for him, everything for the other wrap. He took a beer from the fridge and a bottle of water, paid and turned back to Sigs 2. They started eating and Neil spoke first. "OK, you want the full story and I want some answers from you my old friend. Like why is the plan so important, in the many years we have known each other you have never left London willingly, yet I find you as my contact man in Kiev. I am chasing down a lead from a now dead man in a Chinese teahouse, in the Ukraine. Why are you here? Oh just a thought, don't take that pistol out of your pocket and keep your hands on the table please." These were not pleasantries; they were clear and unambiguous instructions. Sigs 2 tried to shrug these off with a comment about being friends for years. Neil was not sure who was a friend or a foe. He did not and could not trust anyone, except himself. Neil cut him short with a swift jab into his ribs. Sigs 2 coughed up his food. He went pale. "I have had enough of being jerked off and nearly killed too many times to allow you to play the fool. Talk and talk now or you may never make the flight back to your beloved London and your family! This is my area and my turf; don't play clever on my patch, or in my game!" Nobody looked at the figure of a man coughing up his food; the people who walked past assumed he was drunk. Neil passed him a paper serviette. "You bastard" was all Sigs 2 could get out as he tried to control his breathing and slowly turned to face Neil. "I am here trying to save your ass. After that you can fry." "Answer my question you shit. I am in no mood for any crap. Why is the plan so important? What do you know about this new group of people I am hearing about? Who or what is the Network. London did not brief me on you coming to Kyiv! What do you have to do with all of this? Answers now Colin or I mean it you will join the list of officers who never made it through their first field mission." The questions had come fast and cutting. Neil had not called him by his real name in an age and Sigs 2 looked up at him. Neil was calmer and not raising his voice now. Colin knew the signs he was angry, mad as hell, and just as liable to do whatever he threatened. Colin straightened himself up, took a gulp of the beer and looked Neil in the eyes. "I will share with you what I know and it is not much. Then and only then will I tell you that we are finished. No one threatens me, not even you Neil, not even you! I know nothing about the new organisation. I know about the trail of chaos you have left behind from Wuhan. Wuhan station is no more. Madam Lan was the only one to get out alive. Did you see her at the teashop? What are you doing running under the Russian support not ours? Your Russian goon, Eric, keeps me informed. Did you know that Mr? Where did this woman come from and who is she? I cannot find a record of her anywhere. As for the plan, I spoke with top brass before I left London. They are not pleased with you. You are facing a hearing on your return. A possible prison sentence for breaking protocols, murder, theft of departmental funds and directly disobeying orders. Other than that everything is rosy so to speak."

Neil stopped his flow and replied, "Trumped up charges and smoke screens. Tell me what else is going on!"

Colin sighed and ate some of his wrap, which was going cold, "Everyone who has been assigned this route home has never made it. You must have worked that out by now. You are the fieldwork specialist. It is part of the game." Colin had stressed the "You are" and Neil noticed it. He paused and took another drink of his beer, sighed again and continued. "I don't know who, but someone senior wants you out of the way permanently. You were to follow the route your father took and disappear the same way he did. Full honours and mention in the papers, great loss and all that rubbish. Nevertheless, you are to die. I knew your father and he did not die either, he simply got lost. You keep killing off the people who are supposed to kill you. You are not to get lost you are to be killed! They are not our department or section five. They are some outside organisation on contract. Our team know about it on a hush hush basis. Need to know! I cannot even find who placed the contract or how. It is not just above my pay grade. This is a special caveat that will not allow any information released outside of those who hold it. Corrupt, possibly, effective and powerful yes, illegal, most likely, trying to kill you most definitely. This is out of my league and I can do nothing to stop it or to help you. I have said too much already. Last thing I can say is be careful of the last major general." At that point, Colin slumped over the table and fell to the floor. Neil fell with him and checked to see the bullet hole in his back and no exit wound. He got up and waved his hand as if he were saying good-bye to a drunk. Then he swiftly walked down into the metro. The two or three cabin shops protected him from the area where the bullet had been fired, the direction and the general area where his hotel was. He thought about Colin for a brief moment and then wondered about how he was going to get back to the hotel and without being shot. He moved past the florist and thought, *change your persona*. He bought some flowers, red roses and moved towards the main street instead of the subway to the concert hall. He came out of the metro subway and stopped to look at the streets. He decided he would stop and be the tourist. As he put the camera to his eye to take a picture of the concert hall, he saw a man approaching him in the dark screen on the

Canon. This screen only showed picture taken not the picture that would be taken. Neil waited until the last possible moment. He turned the camera and made it flash in the man's face. As he went to cover his eyes, Neil saw the blade in his hand. Neil pushed the camera behind his back and applied the hand twist that he had used successfully in the courtyard. The man countered, forcibly pushing him back. As he started forward towards Neil. Raised a fist to punch Neil on the nose. A police officer stopped and looked at them, saw that the man was holding something, drew his weapon, and fired. That gave Neil the time to run back into the metro entrance. Neil could hear lots of shouting and noise; but he did not look back. He carried the flowers in front of him the man had caught him with the blade and he had not noticed. Blood was seeping through his shirt. He moved swiftly across the forecourt of the metro, which was below the concert hall and walked up the steps. The rain had stopped and the steps were drying. That was something else he had not noticed. Was he getting too old for this? He made the top of the steps, waited, and listened before he walked out into the car parking open area. He surveyed the space and the garages by the right hand side. The building end wall was on the left hand side and the road moving up and away from him was the way he needed to go. No one was on the roof of the garages, and no one could be in the end of the building, unless … He decided to make a move and walked forward with the flowers still in front hiding the blood now covering the front of his shirt. He was not in pain, but he was suddenly tired. His adrenaline levels were dropping too quickly. He made the top of the road, another quick check and he walked up to the back door of the hotel. This was also the entrance to a nightclub. There were a few people hanging around outside and smoking. He avoided the people who were preparing for the nights entertainment and made for the lift. How many knocks did he tell Irina? He got out of the lift at floor four and checked to see that no one was on the terrace. He moved as quickly as he could to the room. Neil was failing and he knew it. Knock twice, then once more. Irina opened the door with a matter of fact glance and said, "For me how lovely." Neil gave her the flowers and collapsed on the floor, holding his waistband. She saw the blood and stopped herself from screaming. Neil dragged himself to the chair and pulled off his shirt, a clean, deep cut across his stomach. Neil hated the word belly. "The small case please Irina." Neil opened the front part of the case and took out some clips. He started to clip the wound together. He must have passed out. The next thing he remembered was lying in the bed and feeling tired. He turned to see Irina, washing her hands and the towel she had used to stop the bleeding whilst she fitted the clips to his wound. It was not large and the clips were working well as the bleeding had stopped. "We will do dinner here tonight please," Neil said to her. She rang the restaurant and ordered food for the two of them. Neil went back to a sleepy state of not knowing what was going on. When he eventually awoke it was light and the food tray had one meal eaten and one not. Irina had found plastic skin in his bag and had sprayed his wound. He was on the mend. He looked over to his right and Irina was still asleep under the duvet. She looked beautiful. "Can this be heaven?" he asked himself.

His mind switched back to what Colin had said and died for saying. Is this why his father had disappeared with no body? Had his father made it out and got away. Why had he never noticed that this route always caused problems? It had never caused problems for him before. He was no closer to understanding what or who was Network. All he did know was that Colin had died because he told him that people at the top of his organisation were involved. Then to be careful of the last major general. Who was he and where was he? How did he have knowledge or contact with the Network? Neil had come to Kyiv to find the house of the man who had tried to kill him in Zhou's teashop. Zhou was dead; Colin was dead, even possibly Madam Lan; this was becoming an undertaker's Christmas party. Irina rolled over and spoke to him, "At last you have woken up!" she said. "Two days you have been asleep or not really awake. How are you feeling now?" Neil found that he was able to move much more easily. The clips were now not attached. "You did all this Irina?" She looked around the room and said; "No one else here but us chickens." Neil moved and pulled her gently to him and kissed her full on the lips. At that moment, even if she was a whore, he did not care. When he broke of the embrace she returned, his kiss and her tongue explored his mouth. Exploring his mouth like it was some mysterious cave. He put his arms around her and held her body close to his, skin to skin, no space between them, only their lips and mouths in a deep embrace. She pushed her hand down his leg into the centre of his body, not touching the wound. *Big boy"* she thought as he moved on top of him and pushed him deeply into her wanting body.

"*Some milk run,"* Neil thought! Then he did not think he was filled with a rush of passion for this woman.

Dinner at 7 breakfast at 7 too

Chapter 8

They got up and he asked Irina. "Can you cope with going out for dinner tonight?" She nodded her head. Separately, but in unison they got ready. She helped him in the shower and he dried and dressed himself. She had bought a gold dress with a panel showing the skin of her back, which she slid into. He put on the standard black suit and leather shoes from his case. They took a taxi to ae restaurant he knew and arrived at seven. Stare Zaporzjzia on Sakaidachnogo Street. Neil suggested, "It is a little cold. Should we dine inside?" They walked up some stairs to a quiet small-secluded dining room with a circular table. Irina had a jacket over her dress, which she took off after they sat down at a circular table and looked at the menu. Whilst they were alone, Neil explained that after dinner, he would take her back to the hotel and then he must go out. Irina forcefully said, "We will see about that." Dinner arrived as ordered, she had fish he had turkey. It was not Christmas but what the hell! The food was good and the company wonderful. He wanted this evening to go on forever. However, he knew it could not. Irina turned to him and asked, "Are you going to the house of the man you were talking about in the apartment?" "Yes I have to follow this up Irina, please go to the hotel; then I know you will be safe." "I will of course not worry about you" she replied and her face changed. "I will come with you. No stronger than that! I am coming with you; you are not fit enough if something happens." Neil knew in an instant that this was not an argument he was going to win. "We'll see after dinner angel." He knew he was starting to feel something very sincere towards this lady. He could not think of that now. He had to work. Irina left to visit the toilet and Neil found himself reflecting on all the different strands of this trip. Some might come together after he had visited the address in Kyiv; some would haunt him to the end of his days, like Colin's death. Others would just drift into, forgotten memories. How could he find out about Network, who was the last or the late Major General, was his father wrapped up in this somehow? Had he really seen him on the London underground? If so, where was he now? Was he still in the game? The last time Neil had to sort out so many variables, he had written the military exercise for a major conflict in Europe. He sat and ascribed different theories to the things on the table. The dead players were a dinner plate, empty and no theory why, the Network was the full water carafe, leadership theory perhaps, the empty glasses, Irina and him that was the prisoner dilemma, and the salt and pepper pots were more unknowns. He moved the items around the table trying to find or think of a link. Something else was missing, his father perhaps? Lost in thought he had not seen Irina return to the room, until she placed her hand on his shoulder and kissed him gently on the cheek. "Playing chess are we? She asked him in a slightly mocking tone. "No just trying to do a bird table." Irina collapsed into laughter at this expression and again mockingly looked for the birds in the room. Neil sighed and gave up; something, another piece of the puzzle was still missing. This game could not be solved easily. Yet, if he failed to solve it, he was dead.

Neil paid the bill and ordered a taxi to drop them at the corner of Volodymyrs ka and Sofiivs ka. They would walk from there. It was a grey night, slight drizzle and a cool wind. The streets reflected the way people were. Heads down, rushing to get out of the weather. Neil suddenly realised that he was dressed for dinner not work. He looked at Irina who was also dressed for dinner. She looked lovely, hair shining and relaxed. They could not change their clothes now. They walked down the road towards the square and turned right into a cul-de-sac. Dark, dingy, with rubbish lying on the pavement as the slowed their pace and Neil cased the apartment block. The joint, what a funny American expression! A door opened in front of them and a couple walked out, heads down. Neil pulled Irina into a clinch and kissed her gently. He thought he heard the man say, "Go get a room." He ignored his comments and broke off the embrace when the couple had turned the corner and were gone. "Right the plan is we are looking for a man who was killed in the debacle earlier to return his things to his family." "Highly original, and what if the is no family and what have you got to give them?" They had reached the end of the cul-de-sac, which was a brick wall; a nightclub bouncer type of man stood outside the door upon which Neil needed to knock. As Neil looked in the gloom there was no door, the man was standing in front of a blank brick wall. Then Neil saw it. It was a rivet and the door was the other side of the wall. He walked up to the side of the man and went for the door. Of course, the bouncer stood in his way. This was not what he hoped for especially with Irina with him. "Where do you think you are going?" the man said. Neil pulled himself up to his full 173 centimetres and said to no one in particular "К черту с! (Sod off!)" The big man was taken back he had not expected this. "I asked where you were going politely" he stuck to his English accent with over tones of Slav. Neil repeated himself and walked forward. The man stood his ground and lifted his hands to a fighting stance. Neil had managed to get himself into the rivet entrance so he had wall by each elbow. Instead of walking any further forward Neil, slowly took out his section 5 card. "Вы понимаете, что это такое вы осла выйти из моего пути сейчас!" "(Do you understand what this is you ass; get out of my way now!)" "That won't get you in here" and then man spat on the ground in disgust. "То это будет," "(Then this will)" said Neil as he sent a crashing backhand chop across the man's throat. He knew that if he had distracted him he could get close enough. The man went purple and clutching his throat sank to his knees, coughing up blood. Neil brought his knee into the man's face and he could hear the crunch of bone, bouncing off the walls. Blood and froth was everywhere as Neil pushed the man aside and ushered Irina to pass him quickly. Neil knocked on the door. A slot opened in a thick wooden door. Neil's hand was through the gap and on that man's throat. "Откройте прямо сейчас! Не заставляй меня просить снова." "(Open it now! Don't make me ask again.)" The man let the catch off the door and Neil pulled his hand back quickly to ensure that no one could pin his hand in the door as it opened. Neil kicked the door and walked in with Irina, eyes wide open, trotting behind him. Neil knew that it had all been too easy as he slowly walked forward into a dimly lit room with a desk, one chair behind it, and two in front of it. This was a set up! Wooden chairs, old, worn but solid hard wood, expensive in their time. He turned his attention to the sides of the room, a bookcase, some books, a worn sofa for two, and another doorway. The light fitting was not well connected and the wires were showing from the ceiling rose.

"Please sit down Neil and, of course, the lovely lady Irina" the voice had come from somewhere behind the desk. At that point, the bookcase moved and man stood there with an Uzi pointing straight at Neil. Neil beckoned Irina to sit down. Nothing to do except play the cards dealt. However, it was still too easy Neil thought. This was worse than playing "Go."

The voice said, "It has taken you a while to get here; but, at last you have made it and you are still alive. A lot like your father, we could not kill him you know. It cost me many dead agents to bring your father in Neil. Did you know he is alive and well?" A bright light shone in Neil's eyes so that he had not seen the man sit down behind the desk. What he could see suggested that he was shortish, stocky, wearing what appeared to be a tailored suit in slate grey, well cut, and finished, silk tie with dragons on the tie, and perhaps a white cotton shirt; good make but Neil could not decide who had made it, possibly hand made. Another dragon tie, was that important? Neil looked at the man's face, as much as he could see passed the lamp. No scars, sharp features, thin lips and no beard, nothing to recognise him again out in the street. Well-spoken in English but a faint accent. This was all he could make out as the glare from the lamp stopped him looking directly at the man.

"Did you know you father is alive and well Neil, or has the cat got your tongue?" "I am terribly sorry I did not catch your name," replied Neil in English. "I came here as an official against a terrible accident in Odessa where a man was fatally injured and this was his only identification, this address I mean. Can you help me and is the man with a gun really necessary?" The man laughed aloud.

Neil was remembering his interrogation training. Interrogation was just part of his job. However, this was not name, rank and number; this was going to be much more difficult.

Neil spoke again, "I am afraid the lady is not part of this inquiry. She is, of course, a gorgeous distraction for dinner. Can we let her go?" "Don't be silly Neil" came the reply. "Why the lady who nursed you back to health would become a distraction. You brought her here from Odessa. The next apartment to your own. Please do not take me for a fool; your father still says that is the greatest mistake in the world to take your opposition for a fool. As far as you are concerned, I am Number 3 and I have a proposition for you. The same one I made to your father, which he accepted in fact. For yours and the lady's benefit, I represent the Network. I, like you Neil, am an executive, although in my case much more profitable than you are. Neil was frustrated. Neil asked, "What do you want?" The reply came back so fast and simple "I want you, with or without the lady Irina, in the Network. You have 24 hours to make a decision and we will meet again to discuss terms and conditions if this business proposal suits." Neil looked down as the bright light shone on his face and into his eyes. He knew the man was gone. He turned and saw that they were completely alone, no man with a gun, no man at the door, nothing and no one.

Neil sat upright, his back as straight as a ramrod. His hands placed on each knee. He was not moving, not his eyes, hands, feet. He sat perfectly still. Was it shock? Was it fear? Neil smelt, for the first time in his life, of fear. It was fear. Neil was not able to grasp the statement about his father. Frightened, he was afraid for the first time in his life. Why, he could not understand? He getting too old for the job? He remembered his mother saying that she had only seen his father afraid once in his life. When he had been caught doing something wrong, as usual, and had to escape upon a coat, hidden in the back seat of a mini motor car on the floor. He could not move he seemed transfixed and then he smelt himself. He stood up and walked towards the doorway. No man there either. Irina followed him. However, she was not sure what to say. Out in the street the breeze helped him with the smell of himself. He could not work out how long they had been there or what would happen next. Neil turned to Irina and said, "I need something to eat please, coffee and some breakfast. Let's find somewhere now!" He also needed a shower but that would wait.

Neil and Irina took their seats in the all night restaurant and ordered a breakfast of scrambled eggs and frankfurters. Neil drank copious amounts of strong black espresso. Until Irina asked, Neil to stop or he would start shaking. He ate slowly and did not speak. He watched the sum rising in the sky over the roof tops of the city. The streaming light seemed to have a positive effect upon Neil and he turned to look at Irina. "I need time to think please. Do you understand? Please go back to the hotel and I will join you there." Neil paid the bill and left after kissing Irina on the forehead. Neil walked down Khreschatyk in the direction of the Indian restaurant "Rimanai." He had dinner there with another blonde-haired woman he remembered. Neil walked up the stone steps and noticed that a van was delivering supplies so the door was open. He walked in and saw the Indian icon on the wall. A smartly dressed woman came towards him and Neil said, "Tell Mr Evans that I need an English lamb curry." "But we are not open sir." "Just tell him please" and Neil took a seat in a booth that looked out over the street. Mr Evans came out from a door across the restaurant. He was a tall and well-built man wearing a white shirt and expensive tailored slacks. He held his hand out to Neil and said *"Waheguru ji ka Khalsa, Waheguru ji ki Fateh"* (The Khalsa belongs to God, Victory belongs to God). Then in perfect English "what brings the scourge of Europe to my humble abode?" "I need to speak with our friends please, can you arrange it quickly?" "My friend, of course I will arrange it immediately. Can I get you something, tea, coffee; do you need food?" Neil looked up at his friend and said slowly and quietly "Just the contact link please." Neil was still fighting his feelings after learning that his father was still alive. How could this be, could he trust the deliverer of this information. He needed to speak with Sigs 2.

However, Sigs 2 was dead. He sat still and remembered that Evans and he had undertaken officer training together. They had shared the pain of the leadership agility tests and never failed on one. Younger men had dropped out or not finished. Evans and he had completed the ten runs, with full kit and the squad. Even when he and Evans could not run from laughing at Wally, their mate and colleague who had stuffed his beret into the mouth of a young recruit trying to impress the directing staff at the top of cardiac hill. The directing staff had also found it extremely funny. Nevertheless, Wally found himself on a charge of "conduct unbecoming an officer" and given extra duties. Neil had hated cardiac hill vigorously and was so pleased when he had completed the runs. He had graduated with Evans and then they parted company for some time. Neil broke from his thoughts by the return of Evans who was every bit a Sikh, resplendent with his turban and necklace of knife, the Kirpan, a comb the Khanga and a Kara, the steel bracelet. The boxer shorts and comb were Neil knew under his trousers and turban. "This way me dear friend, please." Neil followed Evans through a door at the back of the restaurant and into a small room of the lounge, which was empty. Evans gave him a key and said, "Lock yourself in Neil and only unlock if you hear the masonic knock." Neil had forgotten that they had joined the freemasons as well as passing out of officer training together. Neil had lost all sense of time; something he seldom did. He checked his watch it was just before 05h00 in London. He entered the room and locked the door firmly behind him. He sat at the console and put a pair of cans on his head. He used the telephone keypad to dial the number for the Sigs 2 desk in London. It rang and a voice answered, "Sigs 2a, how can I help you?" "This is avenger one" Neil replied. The voice came back and asked, "In clear or scrambled please?" Neil replied slowly and deliberately, "Going to scrambled and add level 3 please." A red light came up on the panel in front of him and then three green lights, before Neil said anything else. "Who is speaking please?" Neil asked. "Sigs 2a" was the reply. "Don't be an ass; what is your name? This is avenger one. Speak up I haven't much time." The voice faltered and then stuttered, "But you can't be. Your under warrant and should be arrested on site. You cannot be on the line. Orders are that I cannot talk to you. You killed my boss." Neil drew breath and said very clearly, "Get the Quartermaster to this line now! Wake him up and tell him it is avenger one. Do it now!" What seemed like an eternity a familiar voice came on the line, "Hello asshole; what have you been up to and why do you want to talk with me?" "Doug it is me Neil." "I don't know whether you should be either in jail or at least on the run. How can I help?" Neil explained what had happened and left no details out, including that his father was alive and some organisation called the Network where all major players. Doug had listened without interjection until Neil finished. "So what do you want me to do? I am the quartermaster here not operations." Neil's answer was simplicity itself, "I trust you Doug find out who the late Major General is for me and send me a coded message as soon as you do. Will you do that for me? Don't believe anything you hear about my actions as they are all untrue." Before Doug could answer, Neil heard the click of a search sweeper activation. All the sounds were so clear in scrambled. He closed the line immediately without hearing Doug's answer. Neil sat back, took the cans from his ears, and watched the lights fade on the console. Neil thought about contacting the Russian's or the Chinese. He thought better of it and walked over the station's safe. He used the universal number and opened the safe, took out a requisition chits and wrote on it. He took out euros, dollars and pounds, as well as two blank passports one French and one blue Ukraine. He took mug shot using the camera install on the console and printed them, affixed them to the passports and sealed them. He put them in the inside pocket of his jacket and pushed the chair back from the desk; having closed the safe door. He checked. Had he remembered to put the chit inside the safe? No sense in a charge of illegal borrowing. Only the British military could have an offence of "illegal borrowing" which implied that the stuff taken might be paid back; therefore, it could not be theft. Neil got up and instinctively switched on the camera to see what was happening before he opened the door. He was surprised to see Evans lying on the floor, badly beaten and a man leaning over him shouting at him. How could people know where he was when he did not tell anyone? Neil pushed a button and sealed the door he had entered. He then pressed another button on the wall panel and watched as the screen went black and then the next image was the street outside of the restaurant. The van was still there; no one was in the driver's seat or near the vehicle. Neil opened the emergency exit by pushing down a red handle next to the console. The door slides silently open and he was able to walk out into the back street above the Khreschatyk Street. The door closed on its own and he walked calmly to the van, opened the driver's door and jumped in. To his surprise, the keys were still in the ignition. I turned the engine over praying that it would fire the first time. It did and he pushed it into gear and drove off. In the rear view mirror, he could see the delivery boy looking amazed and the men standing around a black Merc taking out guns and firing at the back of the van. He turned right and continued into the main street just missing a Zil truck that had just pulled off from the traffic lights. Neil hit the gas pedal and continued without looking back as he turned into the one-way system and jumped the lights; turned right and headed for the hotel. He drove up the hill and turned left into the road to the hotel. He parked in the covered car park and ran up the steps to the back of the hotel. He calmed himself and walked up to the first floor and reception. The receptionist smiled and handed him a letter. "She left sir, no one with her; she just left." Neil took the letter, did not open it; but, turned and pressed the up button on the lift. He opened the room with the plastic key and walked in to see his stuff had been gone through systematically, but checked. His money was still there, but his blank Russian passport was missing, the travel bag was open and the lining ripped open to reveal the "toys." Nothing seemed missing except the passport. Why? Neil packed his things and put everything back into the travel bag. He checked the "toys" too as he put them into the case, grenades, gold coins, knife, spare ammunition, medical kit, wait no gun the Glock was missing. Oh well he never liked the gun anyway. He sat on the white sheets and read the note. "I am sorry but I can't keep up with you, whoever you are. I am going home to face the music for the non-payment of fines and live a quiet life, if I ever can after being with you. I am sorry but I cannot take you anymore. Who the hell are you anyway?" Neil put the letter on the white sheets and thought it was for the best. Things were going to get even stickier. He had less than 24 hours to make up his mind about the Network. Somehow, he had to sort out this thing with his father. He needed to get back to London, not be arrested, and not charged for offences he had not committed. It was decision time. Where to go next, what to do and what decisions should, he take which ones should he avoid? He sat on the edge of the bed and thought about the decisions he had to make. Neil felt pressured into making hasty decisions, which were costing peoples their lives. He did like this feeling or the rushed approach to his work. Irina walked across the concourse of the Kyiv railway station in her high heels and crisp white shirt, open enough to allow the men to obtain just a glimpse of a black bra. The shirt was cotton and crisp and it felt good. She felt good, away from the intrigue and problems. Her black skirt matched the shoes and the stockings were clear and showed her tanned legs. She stopped at the coffee shop and ordered a cappuccino. Paid and took it to a table overlooking the train tracks. She had just settled down to drink her coffee, when a man came up and asked if she had change of a 100 note. She automatically replied, "Try the cash desk." He sat down and looked at her intensely. "You gone native" he asked, "Have you forgotten your job? Why are you here and not with him in the hotel convincing him that his only course of action is to join the Network? Your orders were to lie to him and have sex with him! Instead of teasing men here; get back and do the job you were detailed to do!" The man was well dressed with a sports jacket and an open neck shirt, penny loafers and a pair of light brown slacks. "Who the hell are you to tell me what I should be doing. I run my own scams not you." "I am the man in Network who put you up for this job, groomed you, got the contacts for you to get the apartment next to the safe house and arranged for you to live when the killing spree started. Also for you information my name is David, I am Neil's father. What else do you want to know?" Irina looked hard at the man and for all his style and ability to wear the right things; he was old and looked tired. There was an air about him and a look that resembled the face the Neil could pull when he was lost in thought. "You can't be his father; he is in Paris awaiting the next stage of the plan." David spoke very slowly and very menacingly, "Listen to me very carefully I will not repeat myself for you or anyone else. Get him to Paris as ordered, or I will not be your benefactor anymore and that will mean you will not be the last woman standing. You are alive now because my son likes you I think. The moment that changes and I will know, you become expendable. Do you understand me now Irina?" He threw a few notes on the table and over his shoulder said, "That will pay for your coffee. Do your job or I will do it for you?" Irina looked at the notes and then looked up. The man was gone, not walking down the concourse, perhaps he had dropped down to a platform, but she could not see anyone on the platforms near. How can anyone get lost that quickly? How can anyone disappear so fast and so completely? He was nowhere. David watched her as she left the station and hurried to the taxi rank in front of the main doors. He stood in the doorway, watched her all the way to the first taxi, and saw her jump into it.

Irina could not remember if she had paid for her coffee and did not want to go back into the station just in case. In case of what, the coffee shop was in a public place, open for the world to see, as safe as houses. Oh my God she thought, as safe as houses. No house was safe from these people and Neil did not know it. She had told the driver to go to the Royal Olympic and sat back into the seat. The taxi was just about clean, but the seat belts looked brand new. She had her purse; but the calm and control of the woman walking into the coffee shop was gone. She buttoned up one of the shirt buttons and stopped anyone looking at her bra and her breasts. The drive noticed and took it the wrong was. "Want a detour baby?" "Just drive ass hole," was the reply and he looked back at the road and pushed the accelerator hard to the floor. "Have you just met the man; have you" He scares the hell out of me too and I know him." "What man, what are you talking about, just drive please." "Oh yes! You have met him I can tell by a mile. He said you would come out of the middle door and said your blouse would be one button too much undone, heels and you would be worried. Spot on!" "What are you talking about?" Irina looked at the eyes in the driver's mirror. She did not recognise him or know him. He must be working for the Network, a plant. Jesus they were everywhere. "Just get me to the hotel quickly please." This was a plea not a request. Had Neil had left the hotel, what if he would not accept that she had come back to him, he could easily brush her off? She was dead, she felt like the walking dead, even now. The taxi drove to the lower entrance of the hotel and as she offered to pay the driver stopped her, "Already covered by uncle Dave sweetie, nice rear end too" he shouted out of the open cab window as she ran up the steps and opened the door into the lower floor and the lift. She pressed the button and waited impatiently for the doors to open, she rushed in before the incumbents could leave. They looked at her and walked out as she stabbed at the panel and selected floor four. The lift seemed to take an age and eventually reached its destination, she did not have a key anymore. Foolishly, she had handed it back at the reception with the note. She would have to knock, what if he was not there. Oh, God please let him answer the door please! He had to be there her life depended upon it. Her whole future depended upon it. She hit the door with her fists and pounded like someone in terror. The sound was hollow and as if nothing and no one was in the room. Oh no, it cannot be it cannot be; he must be there!

Neil moved from the bed like a man in a trance, and then he came to his sense and checked the room peephole before he opened the door. He could see a woman too close to make out who she was. "Who is it I don't need the maid service thank you!" "It's me Neil open up please open up" Irina cried out in fear and relief that he was still in the room. Neil heard her banging heavily on the door. Neil opened the door and stood partly in the way and partly behind the door. He looked at her first and then checked the hallway. No one else seemed to be with her or loitering; so he let her into the room. "You left why you are back here? You buggered off! Run out of money or simply could not find another stooge? Sod off Irina and do it now please!" Neil opened the door again and ushered her towards it. "No, no please let me stay please," she was crying and very upset. He did not know why and so he shut the door again and slid the chain across, just in case.

Irina sat on the edge of the bed and floods of tears fell down her cheeks. Her calm and composure was gone. In its place, a mix of fear and hatred came across her face. Neil noticed the change and assumed the hatred was for him. He stayed closer to the bathroom door than the edge of the bed. "Tell me everything if you want to stay alive Irina. I mean it!"

Another man was threatening her, first the father now the son, oh my God! Neil waited until the sobs subsided and the hatred never left her face. Make up running and eye shadow smudged, leaving streaks down her face. Neil offered her his handkerchief and told her to go to the bathroom and wash her face. He would wait until she was able to talk, "but talk you must Irina." He had surprised himself by allowing that last sentence to be said, not just in his head. This whole affair was chaos and a mixture of dumb luck. Everything that could go wrong was going wrong, yet again. He had to get to all of the pieces so that he could sort it out and get home. Irina threw up in the bathroom and when she eventually returned to the bed, she looked awful. She sat perched on the edge of the bed and started crying again. She was scared, scared out of her wits. Would his father give her a chance to kiss and make up or ...? Was it his father or someone pretending to be David? Irina started by asking Neil, "What does your father look like?"

Neil laughed and replied, "Why do you want to know, seen a ghost? I last saw him when I was twelve years old. How the hell would I know what he looks like?" Irina slowed her breathing and replied, "Yes, I have seen a ghost, a man who called himself David your father." Neil moved and sat in the upright chair in front of her. He was getting angry and subconsciously had used the curtains to conceal himself. He suddenly thought the window and grabbed Irina as the pane shattered and a bullet lodged into the wall. If he was getting angry before, Neil was now livid.

He pulled Irina to the floor as a second bullet smashed into the wall. The outside noises clambered into the room and the wind whining from the broken window. As Neil lay on the floor over Irina he thought, shit this is all happening again. More killings, more dead people and I am still the bloody target. He was angry with himself that he got it wrong. He was angry now that he had it so wrong and so many people were dying because of him. How could anyone make a decision in this chaos?

Neil rolled over and waved his hand for Irina to stay down. He opened the back of the suitcase and pulled out a high velocity sniper rifle. It was a Barrett light 0.5, in pieces. Neil put it together, quickly and efficiently. He took a scope and used it to peer back through the hole that was once the window. From the angle of the shot, hitting the wall Neil was able to work out roughly where the bullets had come from. He did this as he loaded the weapon, no stand. He could see a movement in the lens and focused the scope to see how far and what had moved. A man was on the roof of the stadium and partially covered by the plastic domes. Calmly and slowly, Neil stood up using the curtains as cover; he walked towards the gaping hole and with no indication stood in full view. As he did so the rifle was up and tucked into his shoulder, he flicked the aiming device and as the man moved to get a shot. He fired! The rifle the man had been holding fell and clattered over the roof and then came to a stop. The man did not move. Neil had shot him through the forehead, one clear shot and he was dead, another body, another life for what? He waited a moment and then turned and placed the rifle on the bed. Irina got up and ran to him, holding him like he was the last life raft on the Titanic as it is was going down. He let her cry on his shoulder for a brief moment and then pulled her away from him, sat her on the bed and said, "Start talking now!" "I was recruited to work for the Network. I was a hooker in a nightclub in the Crimea.

They offered me a way out of it all. They said that I had to pick up one mark, you! Then make certain that I took you to Paris. They set me up in the apartment next to yours and all I had to do was wait. However, I got into some gambling debts and that was the police officer you saw off." Neil did not reply he just let her talk. "I ran out on you because I was worried that they will kill you and I don't want that on my hands. You are a good man Neil. I never knew about your father, I swear! I know the Network want you, but I do not know why. They set up everything to make it look as if you would never get back to London. I was to leave you in Paris." Neil was not sure how anyone knew about Paris, as Sigs2 was dead. He had kept telling him to use the pre-planned route only. He had not told anyone about Paris, and he sure was not going to tell anyone now he was dead. "I went to a meet at the railway station. I was not going to come back to you. A man, your father said he would kill me if I did not follow the plan. I am scared out of my wits. They tried to kill me without giving me a chance. What kind of people are they Neil?" Neil sat back in the chair and pondered the story. He had no idea of his father's looks, even if he was alive now. He would be 70 something. He looked at Irina and said, "What did this man look like? What was he wearing, did he have cologne on?" That was a plant, as he knew that his father hated perfume of any sort and never wore cologne. Old interrogation habits die hard he thought. Neil knew that his father never wore anything like scent. "How old did he look? Did he have an accent? Tell me the whole thing in detail Irina."

She started to recount the meeting and left nothing out including the manner in which he had disappeared. No cologne, not smell really, well dressed the penny loafers, the sports jacket, and good quality and not worn. He had spoken to her in English and threatened to kill her and do her job if she failed. "Neil, it is my job to get you to Paris, not anything else." Someone was banging on the bedroom door very loudly and shouting did anyone need help. The door opened and the chain held it fast. A hand came around the door and Neil moved and grabbed the hand and twisted it. The shout was clear and the pain was obvious from the shout. Neil opened the door, after checking through the spy hole, and looked at the manager nursing his hand. "You should have given me time to open the door" Neil commented to the party of people outside the room. "What happened, we heard a smashing and saw glass outside. Are you and the lady alright?" Neil was now alert and knew that Irina had come in from the first floor so no one would know she was in the room, except the dead man on the roof. "There seems to be a Network of problems with this hotel during this stay. I take it you are the on duty manager, yes. Then for Christ's sake get it sorted or I will ensure that your reputation will be murdered on the Internet." The manager moved to come into the room and Neil stopped him. "I mean sorted now!" He had picked his words carefully to tell the manager that he knew what was happening and that the manager was not strictly, what he was trying to portray. The man moved back and said something in Ukraine. Neil did not catch it, but returned to the room and shut the door again, bring in the chain across once more. Irina fell onto the bed and was clearly still agitated and deeply upset. "Sorry old girl we need to be somewhere else right now." "Please Neil I can't go outside I will be killed; no, not even for you darling." That last word had slipped out without her realising it. Neil's mind was now in overdrive. Get the cases, put the Barrett back and get out of the hotel and over to the airport. Check the flight times and stay at the airport. When was the Lufthansa flight? Was there a direct to Paris? Could he stop the manager noticing them as he left the hotel? Then he noticed that he was bleeding from the glass shattering and he must deal with that first. Neil tended to his wound and thought that no organisation could hold human life with such little concern and such contempt. Whilst he was thinking Irina had come over and bandaged the open glass cut on his forearm, where he had tried to shelter her. Neil was thinking, and said aloud to no one, "How could my father work for such an organisation?" The question was simple was it his father? Was it a double to make him waver in his resolve? His mother would have known him in an instant but she had died months ago. He had no photographs and no real recollections except his mother's constant nagging about his father. Neil stopped and picked up the telephone called the lobby and said, "Get me a taxi please." "To where please sir?" "That doesn't matter I will pay and tell the driver when he arrives. No wait; tell him to the railway station." Neil hung up and looked at the mess in the room. He was getting angry and that was not good. He needed to get out of Kyiv safely. More importantly, he needed to think the whole thing through and work out what to do next. The man in the house had offered him 24 hours. That was not up yet or was it? How many people were dead because of him? How could he stop all this carnage? There were far too many questions and far too few answers.

Neil picked up the luggage and called Irina to follow him, they took the lift and Neil looked at the roof top bar, which was empty. He thought he saw a shadow move across the rooftop between the chairs, which were off to the left from the window. The lift seemed to be taking an age. Neil looked up again and saw the shadow again coming closer. He waited until the last possible moment, still not lift. Neil opened the door with force and smacked the shadow, a man in the face with the door. The man's nose erupted and started to bleed as he shouted "I am the bar man and what the hell was happening I was coming to get ice.

Neil calmly said, "Yes you need it for your nose"; then walked forward into the open lift and pushed the button for floor two.

Irina said, "That was not helpful hurting the staff." Neil ignored her and was worried about the lift opening into the reception area, a wide-open space. No one was in the lift area as the doors opened. Neil walked out carrying the two suitcases, with Irina behind him. He moved to the reception desk and asked to check out please. The manager was hovering. He moved quickly away as Neil stared at him. "A taxi was ordered" Neil asked in English. "Da da, yes yes "and the receptionist pointed to the main doors. Neil paid in cash and turned to the main door. Irina took one piece of the luggage and Neil picked up the other. They walked down the steps covered in the red carpet and the driver got out of the taxi. His window was open, but it had turned coldish. Neil put the cases in the boot of the car, whilst Irina got into the car on the passenger side. Neil had noticed that she had noticed the driver. He was a young fit and Neil supposed a good-looking man. Irina had smoothed her dress down and adjusted her hair, as a way of coping with the fact that he was the taxi driver from the station. As Neil opened the door behind the driver's seat, he noticed that the driver had his seat belt on. Most Ukraine men saw that as being a wimp. Neil turned to Irina and said, in English "Please put your seat belt on; something is not right." Irina looked up and adjusted the seat belt. She was looking out of the car and anyone near them. There was no one near. Neil had checked the steps up to the President's hotel and could see no one. He was too used to trusting his instincts to ignore anything at this moment. The driver still had the window open and ignored Neil's request to shut it. As they car moved off, Neil could see a man at the cash machine by the bank and a motor bike parked by the railings. He was seemingly getting money out, and had his back to the car. As the car moved down the slope to the join the main road, just before the steps to Hotel Rus, the driver braked hard. The driver, thrown forward at a great speed stopped himself from crashing through the windscreen, by the seatbelt. Neil was even more worried. As the taxi set off again, Neil noticed a man standing on the steps to the hotel Rus with a laptop in his hand. Suddenly the car slowed down and crawled along. Neil shouted at the driver to get on with it and go to the airport. A motor cycle came past the car's open window and fired an air pistol through the window. Neil could clearly see the feathered dart sticking in the man's neck as his hands fell from the steering wheel. The car increased its speed, even though the driver was no longer able to control anything. The car went down the hill, braked hard, pulled out in front of the traffic, and then moved across to turn left and enter the other side of the carriageway. Horns were sounding and people waving their hands. Neil tried to move the man, but could not as the speed of the car was erratic and kept throwing him about in the back. Irina was screaming. The car went around the one-way system, passed the Royal hotel De Paris and turned into Tarasa Shevchenkas Boulevard. It pulled over and came to a stop in front of the church by Leontovycha. Neither door could be opened nor the windows either. Neil was worried and trying to think what would happen next when a voice echoed in the taxi. A voice that seemed vaguely familiar. "Neil you and Irina will get into the car parked in front of you then and drive to Boryspil. You Neil will take the Air France flight to Charles De Gaulle. Irina will take the car to the Network car parking Zhuliany; she knows the way. I will have control of the car all the way, so any attempt to drive anywhere else will be futile. Do you understand? If so, then answer me please; I can hear you." Neil retorted, "If you can hear me then open the doors the smell of a dead man is making me gag." He was playing for time, which he knew he did not have. "Neil don't try and run or Irina will be shot before she gets to the car. Yes that's it the black Merc!" at that point the doors were opened and Neil got out, went to the back of the taxi and opened the boot; slowly took out his bags and shut the boot down hard. Nothing, he could not see anyone, the traffic was passing by as normal, no police, no walkers, nothing just the Merc in front of the taxi. Irina was visibly frightened; she had recognized the voice as the man from the railway station, who had told here to do her job or die. She said nothing to Neil. Neil moved to the Merc and put his bags on the back seat. He had tried the boot, locked. He got into the driver's seat and Irina got into the passenger's side and closed the door. "I suppose you can still hear me?" Neil asked after the doors closed. "Of course" came the reply. "Then who the hell are you?" Neil's head was rotating more than a fighter pilot on his first bounce mission. He could not see anything or anyone that might be in contact or control of the car. The care pulled away, having indicated first and drove towards the roundabout at Peremony, turned and came back up Shevchenka and then headed towards the bridge and the airport. Irina had said nothing, but was shaking and sobbing. He could smell her fear, rotten and unpleasant. He did nothing and just waited. Neil could not talk with her, as they would be overheard. Then he thought of a line of questions that would not matter if someone over heard. "So you work for the Network too?" "Yes" she replied in a monotone voice. "You were sent to set me up, I take it" "Yes!" she started crying, put her hands over her face and then in temper shouted "Shut up just shut up." Neil noticed that the motorway was not busy. He asked to no one in particular, "What time is this flight? Have I sufficient time to book in and get a ticket?" The same voice came back with, "Go to the Air France desk and pick up your ticket and we will meet in Le Chien qui Fume, you know where that is I take it?" "Yes I do! And I should ask for whom please?" "The table is reserved for the old man. Is your French up to that?" "Yes asshole, who are you?" "We will meet in Paris. Oh by the way, if you fail to arrive in Paris Miss Irina will fail to remain alive. So it is up to you Neil and only you!" The remainder of the drive to the airport was uneventful. Silent and as Neil got out at the departures entrance Irina moved across and kissed his cheek. She took his place and as soon as the bags were out, the car indicated and moved off. She did not look back. Neil stood alone looking at the terminal building. The Network person had lied. It was not 24 hours since his meeting and they had offered him 24 hours to decide. His thoughts turned to the car disappearing into the traffic. Would he ever see her again? Did she really care? Was she just worried for herself? What would the Network do to her, if anything? Yes, she was a Network agent and had set him up. She had felt close to him. He was a mix of thoughts and feelings.

All roads lead to Paris – Even the Ones that Don't

Chapter 9

Another voice called his name. "I am your chaperone Neil. I am deaf, but you do not need to shout and pull mouth faces. I am deaf not daft or stupid. Please come this way." "Are you travelling with me to Paris? Neil asked. "No just to see you onto the flight; that is all, Oh and please carry your own bags. I do not substitute for a porter, I am afraid." The man waited until Neil had picked up his bags and ushered him into the Departure lounge and to the Air France desk. Neil dropped into French, "vous avez une réservation pour moi, docteur Taylor. Oui, non? Neil c'est moi, pour voler à CDG" (You have a reservation for me, Dr. Taylor. Yes or no? Neil it is me. To fly to CDG). "Eh bien oui docteur Taylor, sans aucun doute, de première classe unique de Charles De Gaulle. Veuillez-vous rendre sur le bureau et la main déposez vos sacs. C'est un plaisir pour vous de voler avec nous docteur Taylor." (Well yes Doctor Taylor, without a doubt, first class single to Charles De Gaulle. Please go to the baggage drop your bags. It is a pleasure for you to fly with us Doctor Taylor.) Neil walked over to the baggage drop with his escort, who smiled but said nothing. He asked and received an aisle seat as usual and then walked back towards the entry for departure. "You coming through as well" he asked the man. Neil stopped and looked at him for the first time. Tall, well taller than he was, square shoulders and a straight back; a well cut suit and black loafers. Either all of a sudden, loafers were becoming very popular or the Network members wore only loafers. Neil looked down and realised that he had his black lace ups on not his loafers. His phone rang and he answered it. "Was the weather good in Kiev?" "Not really" Neil replied and then said, "How is my mother these days?" He turned to the man and mouthed my brother. It was Sigs2's replacement, he could tell from the question and the speech of the man on the other end. "She is not too good in herself these days. She wonders if you are ever coming back to London to see her." Neil replied in a throw away manner "I have to stop off in Paris first and then I will be home tell her, I am sorry for the delay." "Good news that you are on your way? Some little filly in Paris I suppose?" Neil laughed and replied" Jeff you know me too well." Neil hung up and looked at his chaperone who was looking intently at someone near the entry to the restricted flight area. That man wearing black glasses, hearing aids, and carrying a white stick was trying to negotiate the full body X-ray machine. Poor sod, thought Neil until he saw that the man was also wearing black loafers. The chaperone waved a pass at the blonde haired girl stamping boarding cards and he went through first. Neil decided that a bolt for it was not a good idea, so he meekly went through the search procedures. He replaced his belt, put stuff back into his "on-board" bag and went forward to the shop on the right hand side. "Need to pick up something for my mother," he said as he walked over and picked up a set of Russian dolls. He was riding his luck; the man had not done his homework. His mother was dead. At least someone was trying to monitor him in London. His telephone rang again. "Section 5 deputy head sir, may I ask where are you." He was speaking in English, very odd. "I am on my way to Paris if it is any of your concern. I will make contact when I arrive. Do not disturb me again." That was the signal for the man at the other end to keep track of Neil's movements. "I am so sorry to have disturbed you. May I ring you in Paris please as something has come up? My senior asked me to tell you that number one does not wear loafers. Does that mean anything to you?" "Yes, but not now" Neil hung up. He was lying of course. He had no idea what was the man talking about. Still it would make sense in the fullness of time. The word had gone out to the Brits and the Russians together. All he could do was hope that the rest of the Network was as poorly informed as this chaperone.

Neil ushered through customs and immigration. The guard stamped his passport and the tall man was still close to him. As they came out the other side, Neil moved over to a seat near the toilets. He turned quickly grabbed the man by his lapels, who tried to move back. His shoulder's fell back and came forward as Neil head butted him and knocked him out. Neil turned him around, placing him on a chair, picked up his own bag and walked away as if the man had never been anything to do with him. Neil moved quickly to the end of the terminal and went down the escalator. At the bottom, he checked the board and went to gate D 7. The flight was boarding and he moved to the business and first class boarding gate. It was then he noticed that the man in the wheelchair, hearing aids, and dark glasses was boarding the flight in front of him. Neil walked slowly so as not to disturb the old man in the chair. Pulling his bag behind him and waited whilst the wheelchair turned towards a first class seat. Neil hated window seats and sat in the aisle. He looked across and saw the old man in an aisle seat two rows behind him. Neil checked that no one sat behind him or near him. First class was empty, save for two men the old, blind and deaf man and himself. The plane was ready for take-off and Neil had not seen the tall man again. Neil settled himself and closed his eyes. He was not happy and not comfortable. He tried to sleep during take-off. That was something that his mother had told him his father always did. Neil was thinking a great deal about this strange man, who he could not remember. Neil would not know him if he saw him. This was stupid and not allowing him to consider the situation. His father was dead. Neil aroused from his thoughts when a pretty air flight attendant offered him a drink. "Non merci!" Neil closed his eyes again and almost instantly, he heard a noise. He turned around to see the old man had dropped his drink and was clearly upset about the mess … Something was wrong, what was it? Neil looked again and then realised that a blind man would not know what the mess was or where it was, unless he had tipped stuff onto himself. The drink was over the air flight attendant and not on the blind man. Neil looked hard at the old man. Well dressed, tailored jacket and slacks, silk tie and cotton shirt and brown loafers. The old man had drawn out a white cotton handkerchief and was dabbing his face as if the drink had splashed him. His face was dry, before the cotton square had gone near his face. The plane was taxiing and the flight attendant, moved to the front of the plane and sat down, buckled herself in and the old man sat quietly. Neil turned back to stare in front of himself and his mind was racing. More loafers, more intrigue, more of the Network on this plane as well? The aircraft taxi and took off with a rolling start as it turned onto the piano keys of the runway. The flight was on and Neil felt a wave of calm come over him as the aircraft rotated and left the ground. It banked sharply and Neil wondered if something was wrong. No, just turning back because of the take-off runway. The light remained on for seatbelts for a long while. Neil always waited for the seat belt to go off and then a nervous dash to the toilet. He was not afraid of flying; but he did not enjoy it as much as his mother had said his father did. His father had be taught to fly a jaguar aircraft in the famous 14 Squadron when he was their "Int officer." His mother had told him about the time she complained because the men on the squadron had referred to his father as "Squint" and she thought they were being rude about his eyes. One of the pilot's had explained that it was a term of endearment and a shortened from of Squinto or Squadron Intelligence Officer. Neil wished that he had known his father; that perhaps he was not all bad; he had served his country for a long while and would have been an old man now. An old man who had poor eyesight and perhaps hearing loss from working with airplanes. Strange that this old man also had hearing loss and bad eyesight. That was strange. He had no pictures of his father; his mother would never have allowed it. He really did not know what he had looked like. Neil turned his attention to the problem at hand. What was he going to do about the Network? What was he going to do about Irina? What was he going to do about London and the mandarins? His additional sources had suggested to him that the world order would now change with the Russian link and the Chinese link; how was he going to explain that these links had kept him alive in the past. Oh, to hell with it he could explain that somehow! The "Trolley Dolly" served the food and for aircraft food, it was quiet good. "Sexist comment," Neil thought to himself. He was normally never sexist. "I must get a grip!" Neil looked at the old man with a spoon. A young woman, who had appeared from behind the grey curtain, helped him. Neil stopped feeding his face as he caught sight of the woman's face. Was it? It was Irina. No, she would not have had enough time to get from one airport to Borispol and board the flight. Was it possible? He had not seen the people boarding as he was almost the last to enter the aircraft. She was soberly dressed in a grey skirt and white blouse and was feeding the man as if she had nurse training. Neil smiled to himself; this organization was a piece of ... He stopped himself from swearing, his grandmother had always said it was a sign of a limited vocabulary. The flight seemed to be passing off without much upset. However, he had not managed to sort out the problems. The flight would be over soon and he needs to ensure that he found a hotel and then decide if he was going to the restaurant. That was Irina, he could tell as she moved back behind the curtain and the sway of her hips. Neil thought back to holding her close and the touch of her skin on his own, soft and gentle caresses and deep passionate kisses. "Oh knock it off" he told himself. Get back to business. Was she supposed to distract him? That woman was doing that, even if it was not her. Neil opened the small case of the matching luggage. This was all he had now; the one bag and its hidden tricks and support stuff. He checked that a flight attendant was not looking his way and was fussing with the old man. Who was also not looking his way? He slipped a small lever in the top of the case and a tray opened up with a variety of passports and identity papers. He selected a French id card and passport and slipped the light blue passport of a Ukrainian citizen in its place in the tray. He checked his wallet and ensured that besides the Ukrainian Ghrivas, he also had Yuan, euros, dollars and English pounds. He was not short of money, even though he had not visited a bank in some time. He had picked up enough on his way around. The old man seemed to have a coughing fit and did not look too well, when Neil turned to see what was going on again. He was trying to stand and seemed to have caught himself on the tray, which was still down. Funny if he had put the tray down, a blind man would have remembered it and felt for it, not just stood up. Neil was now certain that the old man was not blind. I wonder if he is deaf as well, Neil mused to himself. Neil shut up the tray, did not notice that another flight attendant, leant over him, and was trying to remove his British passport from his case. He shut the tray and caught her fingers. He placed the ID card and his wallet in his inside pocket of his jacket, swore at the flight attendant. He slipped his jacket on and adjusted his seat belt. The old man was sitting down now and was adjusting his seat belt as the seat belt light was illuminated. Was the flight really over this quickly? He called a different air flight attendant over and asked, "What was happening?" "We are on approach to Charles De Gaulle" she said, Neil sat back and relaxed. He did not see the other flight attendant come up and fall onto him. He did feel the needle go into his arms through his jacket and then his head swim as he passed out. The aircraft appeared to drop and then righted itself. The captain came on the tannoy system and explained that the turbulence had passed and passengers should keep their seat belts on whilst seated. Irina came through the grey curtain and stood there to stop anyone following her. The old man moved easily and quickly removing his dark glasses and replacing them with a pair of bi focal. He had never been able to cope with varifocals, even though he had needed them. He mused to himself that the last time he had tried them he was driving and had become positively dangerous. He moved over to the limp and lifeless body of his son. David looked at him and said to no one in particular. "That was a long time you ass; too long and now?" He let the words hang in the air for a moment and then signalled for the stewards to get to work. The air flight attendants changed Neil's clothes, put a pair of dark glasses on his face, and placed hearing aids in his ears. The old man took his calf leather wallet. No one spoke and Irina stood watching as the flight attendants transformed Neil into David and David into Neil. David took the bag and pulled the lever, opened up the tray and placed the passport and ID back in the tray. He checked his own passport and French ID card. He reread his Direction de la protection et de la sécurite de la defense DPSD) and then placed it back into his own black leather wallet. David sat on the arm of the aisle seat opposite the seat his son was now occupying. He looked long and hard at him. He son was well dressed, hair neat and tidy, clean nails and no facial hair. He was propped up in the seat and his seat belt was tightly fastened so that if he moved he would not get hurt. David took Neil's seat and asked for an espresso coffee. Irina stood beside him and asked what should she do? "Sit next to him and calm him when he wakes up. We will be in Paris in about an hour. Silly he did not check the time on his posh Skagen watch. Oh well, we all make mistakes." David mused to himself, how many more mistakes would Neil get away with before he was taken out once and for all. He, David, had been the last man standing on many occasions and now he was looking at the prospect of it being his son or him. Could he go through with his order if he had to? He had been ordered to kill Neil if he turned down the offer to join the Network. How can any man kill their own child, even a child he had not seen for over 25 years? What was it he had said to so many other parents "a man or woman should never have to bury their child"? But that was an issue he would have to deal with if Neil turned down the offer. If … … … David closed his eyes and sat still for what seemed like an age. He reflected upon some of the field experiences he had undertaken for Queen and country. All the time he had put his life on the line to be told by some mandarin that his time was over and after his final trip home he would be to fly a desk. He had been told that he was too old and he would be asked to teach the subject to young intelligence officers. Gone was his skill at analyzing the situation, his ability to look at the big picture and get it right time after time. Gone was his skill at languages and ability to be the grey man. Yet, none of his abilities had gone; the office was just not going to use him and make way for some snotty kid. He would not and did not accept it; that was why he took the Network job when it was offered. No one at home, in the West, single if anyone asked, after the last divorce and only one child who acknowledged him. He had even made love with a few ladies. He had never liked the idea of just sex. David remembered that once he had been used for a one night stand, very enjoyable at the time; but, he felt used and abused and sent home come the morning; an odd feeling of not being worth much to anyone. He had felt that way most of the time now and he really did not like it. He wanted to have the buzz of being useful of working out problems on a scale that many others could not. He wanted to be back in the real game, not this game of recruitment and no action, no real action! His son stirred in his sleep and David look over at him and thought about the lost and wasted years of not being a father, to his only son. Why had his son, his only son, gone into the game; surely his mother had tried to dissuade him, surely? He had hoped that his son, his clever dyslexic son would have made something of himself, a lawyer, accountant something to make some money. He had not known what he had done for all those years, until number one had come to him and said that he must recruit him for the number three position as number three was to be rested, killed! The tannoy systems called we are on final approach, he checked that Irina was looking after his boy and checked his own seat belt and adopted the position hands on his legs and back straight, belt tight. The landing was alright and the taxi to the bay was uneventful. As soon as the walk way was connected the captain explained that a passenger had suffered an illness in the forward part of the airplane and disembarkation would take a little longer. A medical team came in and Neil was placed on a trolley and Irina went with him as they wheeled him out of the aircraft in a sit up trolley. David walked slowly out of the plane, straight back and no dark glasses, looking for the world a lot like his son.

No Parent Should Have to Bury Their Child"

Chapter 10

David saw the ambulance move away from the aircraft side of the terminal and then moved towards his favourite black Citroen C4, leather seats, wing mirrors that folded back, headlights that followed the road. Citroen knew how to make good cars. When he had lived in France, all those years ago, he had a Citroen. David gassed up the C4, drove from the airfield. He moved out into the traffic flow and headed for the periferrique. He would drive to Issy and then turn off to get to his apartment in Meudon. For someone who had disappeared he had always thought it funny that his apartment was behind the police station. He had good relationship with everyone in the shops and the local police. No one really knew him, except his Chinese wife. That was by design. He smoothly moved lane and pushed the accelerator down. Suddenly he did not want to be near the airport; he wanted to be at home, alone and give himself time to think. As the darkness started, the lights on the car came on automatically. Traffic was not too bad this time of the evening. He knew the Network would take Neil to the special hospital controlled by them and he could start the process in the morning. Irina was with him, and he was safe from any British, Russian, or Chinese interference.

David was fighting to stop himself thinking about Neil's mother. She was a beautiful woman and had brought Neil up well. Why had she allowed him to go into the game? He was so busy reflecting upon this he almost missed his turn. The sounds of car horns blared as he pulled over the lanes and turned off the periferrique. The rest of the journey was on "autopilot." No the car was not that clever. David did not think about much he just drove. He pulled into the car park in front of the apartment block, maison rouge. Home many were there in France. Any way he locked the car and walked up the stairs to the glass doors. They had finished repainting the outside. What an expense! He opened the door and walked into the entrance, checked his mailbox, nothing, and opened the door and turned to his apartment. He checked the door and the small wooden pick was still in the side of the door. Well old habits die-hard. He pulled it out and opened the door. Shutting the door, he went to pull the curtains before he put the lights on. The shutters remained closed, even in summer. The cleaner had been in and the polished floors were clean and showed no marks. David took off his outdoor shoes and put on slippers. The hung up his coat and moved into the kitchen, turned on the Nesperesso machine and made himself a strong coffee. He took the small bowl of espresso coffee into the lounge and sat down on the futon. He did not turn on the television or the radio. He pushed a switch and the stereo started up. He had programmed Chopin's Nocturne in E first then some Michael Bolton and next some Mozart. He relaxed and slowly drank the hot coffee. He sat and listened to the most beautiful music in the world. That was his opinion of the nocturne. He had been alone for a long while since he had moved from China for this job, and although he could live with himself; he did need female company from time to time. Like the lady, his wife, he had found in China. He ought to visit her. He missed her, but she understood. Various other women came into and out of his head. David was no monk and never intended to be so as he sat and relaxed. He thought about his blood pressure. The medic had given him hell on his last check-up. He did not care. He had put his blood pressure up when he started in the game to allow him to be able to cope. He had never learnt negative feedback to bring it back down. He would die one day but not tonight. He fell asleep on the futon and slept deeply for the first time in a long, long while, longer than the usual four hours. His sleep was deep and gentle no turning over and wandering around the futon. If he had, he would have fallen off. He woke, got up and walked to the bathroom. He put the light on and looked at the face starting back at him from the mirror. That man had lines on his face, sagging jowls and his hair was starting, at last, to go white. He brushed his teeth, which had never been white and washed his face with hot water. He then applied the Vita Lift 5 and put the container back on the rack. He undressed and looked at his body in the mirror. No real scars, except the one across his stomach. How he hated that word belly. The cream felt good on his skin and he would leave it to dry in before he shaved. He showered and looked at his feet as the water ran down his tired body. How could he be tired when he had slept so well? Stress always made him tired. Go for the vitamin B tablets before breakfast and another coffee.

At the same time David was waking up his son was also waking up in the "hospital." Somewhere in Paris, he was in a hospital bed and Irina was sitting next to the bed. She was asleep and her head was on the side, allowing her blonde hair to fall over her eyes. Neil looked over to her and though that she was beautiful, lovely skin, blonde hair, beautiful eyes and a good figure. She had sold him out; she had set him up for the Network. She was no better than many of the women he had encountered. Was she any worse? His head was hurting and he wanted an espresso. He tried to move and found that he was strapped into the bed with leather straps across his legs and chest. He could move his hands and head, but not much else. The inside of his mouth tasted badly, it was dry and he wondered what chemicals they had put into him to knock him unconscious. Neil did not approve of chemical medicine. He could not work out why he was so against them. His mother had always used chemical medicine when he was ill as a child. He never felt good pushing chemicals into his body. He lay back and thought of what could he do tied up here and what would happen to him. He knew nothing about the Network and did not know if he believed that his father was alive or dead. He simply did not know. Irina's head fell forward and she woke up. Neil turned his head and look at her as she slowly rubbed her eyes. She was wearing a nurse's uniform and it fitted in all the right places. Now was not the time to think about relationships or sex. He need to get out of this mess and sort out what he wanted to do and why. Irina, leant over him and her breasts brushed across his chest ad she undid the leather straps. Having released the chest strap she turned and released the legs straps. Neil stayed still until she had released the last strap. Then with speed, Irina had never seen he was up and had his hand around her throat. She was coughing and trying to drag his hand away. Drugged he may have been yet; his ability to react quickly had not diminished. He held her for a moment and then let her body crumple into the chair. She was gasping for air. Neil looked around for clothes and the door. He had no idea what was the other side of the door or where he was. His reaction was to get out and regroup. He frantically looked for something to wear rather than go out into the world outside the door with his rear end exposed. Irina stuttered that she would help him, if he did not hurt her. "You sold me out bitch! Why should I believe you anymore?" Neil stopped himself he did not refer to anyone by using such rudeness. He turned to look at her and she was sobbing. Deep, sincere sobs of pain and personal hurt. "I had to, I had to they threatened to kill me. Your father told me so in Kyiv." "In Kyiv, when did you see my father? Oh when you left. How do you know it is my father? What did he look like speak up"? Neil was angry, frustrated, they had gone over this before and he still had his rear end uncovered. He sat back on the table and waited for her to reply. Irina was sitting crumpled and still sniffing back tears. He had not hurt her too much when he had grabbed her throat. He had used her closeness to check. He was certain that she had a gun under her nurse's uniform; yet, she had not attempted to use it on him. Perhaps she was not too much of a turncoat. As he sat there waiting he looked at her breasts, firm and the nipples were erect, even though she was upset. He was concerned about the effect she was having upon him. He was getting excited with few clothes and her tight fitting uniform was having an interesting diversion for him. She moved the chair closer to him and she paced her hand upon his thigh. He did not stop her. He wanted information from her and would do whatever it took to get the information. She stopped sniffing, sobbing, and looked into his eyes. She softly said, "I have felt something for you since we met. I had to do what they told me. My sister's daughter's life is at stake. "Oh that old chestnut" said Neil. "No it is the truth, I assure you it is." "Tell me about my father and your meeting Irina please?" "I saw him at the railway station in Kyiv. He looks very much like you. No you look like him I suppose. He is very good looking for his age. He must have been attractive in his youth?" Neil replied, "How the hell would I know." He bit his tongue, as he had not meant to break the flow of her thoughts. Irina seemed to have not heard him she was going to continue. "He asked me about you, well sort of. He told me that if I did not follow the plan his own hand would kill me. He really frightened me and I believed him. He is very intense man.

He is well spoken, does not wear any cologne or aftershave. He smelt nice. You don't wear any aftershave do you Neil?" She was lost in her own thoughts and Neil was not ready to play father confessor to her over his own father. He did not care if he smelt nice or not. He knew that his father had been one of the best killer's in the department; everyone had said so when he joined. This was going nowhere and his rear end was getting cold where the edges of the gown did not cover. "OK Irina, give me one good reason not to leave you here and just get out whilst I can?" "You can't go they will bring you back and you will get me into more trouble." "Why should I worry about that? You set me up and let me fall into your trap. Thank you very much. What is this rubbish about your sister's daughter?" She was stroking his thigh and he could not completely concentrate. He knew now was not the time for her to seduce him. Although he wanted to feel her close, very close. He stood up and let her hand fall from his leg. "Can you get me some clothes please?" "No, I told you they will blame me."

It was too late as the door opened and an old man came into the room. He was upright and strode forward with confidence. Neil did not like the look of this as he felt he had missed his chance to escape. "So young man we meet after many years." Neil looked up and took a long hard look at the old man. He looked similar to himself, but older. His hair was still a natural colour, a few white hairs, or was it dyed? He stood upright and erect, wearing a loose fitting suit, but tailored to his shape, loafer shoes black and highly polished. He worn spectacles and had hearing aids in his ears. He shut the door and turned back to face Neil. Neil looked hard and eventually decided that the man did resemble him slightly. Did he resemble the man slightly? "Who the hell are you and what do you want with me" Neil felt offense was the best defence in this situation. "Sit down; shut up you might learn something." His grandfather would say. "I am number two in the

Network and I am also your father. References to my death are much exaggerated. I am pleased to say. I will explain everything if you shut up and listen. Do you wish to learn what is happening or do you want to talk?"

Neil did not know what to respond to first; his father, the number two to this mystery organization that was trying to kill him, listen to what, why? Questions thundered in his head. None of which he could answer.

Neil stopped himself and found he was asking the following question "Does Uncle Jeffrey know you are alive, you arsehole?" "I am your father; I would appreciate it if you did not refer to me as an asshole; even if you have not bothered to find out about me. But I expect that is because of your mother, rather than anything else." "How can you find out about a dead man asshole?" David's arm came up and slapped Neil's face. "Last time I raised my hand to you, you complained that I was violent. You don't know anything and perhaps you have not learnt anything in the time we have been apart?" Neil felt rage come up inside him, rage that followed the arguments that his mother had lodged in his brain from a child about his father and how bad he was. As far as Neil was aware, his father had never raised his hand to a woman; he had smacked him as a child. As for David, he remembered his father smacking his face because he had been rude to his mother; only once; their lives followed similar paths; yet each failed to tell the other.

There was a long silence and tension great tension between the men. Eventually Neil said, "What do you want?"

David drew breath and stood his full height, which was shorter than Neil was. The scene could be funny, him dressed, Neil in a smock and Irina as a nurse. "This could be a London farce," Neil said to no one in particular. David opened his mouth and started to speak after waving his hand for the both of them to sit down. "Network wants you to take over as number three and then replace me eventually. I am supposed to turn you and set you up or kill you. Yet, a parent should never have to bury his child. Military training Neil remember. Irina stirred and Neil saw her involuntarily go for the gun. "Don't do anything silly Irina, not just yet anyway. Hear me out please' both of you. I have no desire to kill either of you and especially not my only son. Equally I believe that another of you really know anything about Network. I will fill you both in on the last part the Network and then I have a plan for us all to get out in one piece. Are you prepared to listen and learn something?" Irina looked at Neil, looked at David and did not know what to say or do. She felt for Neil, perhaps even loved him; yet, she was frightened of his father, very frightened. As she turned towards David, he said to her, "Give Neil the gun. He is a better shot than you, and take the nurses uniform off and put on a jumpsuit in the draw under the table. Do not touch the buttons on the side. Please do not go for false modesty. This already looks like a Whitehall farce and I have no desire to keep it going any longer. Both men looked as she took off the uniform and slide into the jumpsuit. It fitted perfectly and covered all of her curves. She was a very attractive woman. Neil then said, "OK where is something to cover my rear end?" The next draw, do not touch the buttons. The button on the left will open a door and two flights down is my Citroen black C4. That is the escape route for us all." Neil opened the draw and took out all the necessary clothing he would require, underwear, jacket and trousers and a pair of brown loafers, with tassels. Neil pulled on the underwear prior to taking off the medical robe. He quickly dressed and put the silk tie on and checked his attire. "You thought of everything thank you David." "I am telling you this as your father, the next thing to remember is that if anyone comes in from the door I entered shoot them and get out? I will be there with you. OK? David tapped the floor, a stool rose up, and he sat down. He still had the confidence and calm, no weapon and no bump under his jacket to suggest it. Neil sat on the table and looked down at his father. He suddenly seemed an old man, who was tired and drawn. David did not give way to anything. He just started explaining the Network. "The Network is an organization that believes that governments' are not the best group of people to control and manage world peace. They formed many years ago when the United Nations' could do little about world powers pulling the strings of other nations, primarily the Russians, the Americans and the Chinese. A committee of people runs it from a few nations such as France, the UK and Malaysia. You have met number three and I am number two. Number one is the late major general and French, Malaysian, and Russian operatives hold the remainder top jobs. Some very wealthy backers who never surface pay for the Network. Money is never the object. World peace is the mantra! Still with me? The problem is that the Network is concerned with the Russians, which is where you come in son." Neil thought that sounded odd, calling him son. "We need to talk outside of this situation. Can we get out of here?" Neil looked down on his father. He was a good six inches taller than he was. "Are you really my father?" "Yes I am; but you managed to keep apart from me for a long while." David's face changed for no apparent reason. "This room is not wired; however, they will be here soon. Open the escape door and get down to the car now please." When this man spoke, people listened, both Neil and Irina listened, and Neil pushed the button to see the table he had been sitting on slide to one side and a staircase open up. Clothed and now clear-headed Neil started down the stairs, and then turned "Are you coming as well." "I will be with you in a few moments, get into the back of the car." David was gone. Neil saw the entry door slide shut. Where had he gone? Had he gone to betray them? Irina pulled at him and whispered for them to go down the stairs. The stairs were clinical and metallic. They went down for a short while and levelled off into a walkway, well light and no apparent cameras. The walk way ended in a shiny metal doorway. Neil had no idea what was the other side, where they were and how high up they were. His hand faltered on the door handle. It was really a lever. What would happen if he lifted the lever and recapture greeted them? He slowly lifted the level fully. No bells, no alarms rang and no flashing lights. Irina stood next to him and he could feel the tension and heat from her body. He did something he had never done before when he was working. He stopped and turned, pulled her to him and kissed her sensuously on the lips. She did not pull away from him; in fact, she did the opposite. She came closer and he felt her shape push against him. She was hot and seemed to meld into his shape, as if her every contour seemed to fit into his shape. Oh, if he had the time, because, he definitely had the inclination. Eventually, after what seemed like a long time, Neil pushed her back slightly and pushed open the door. Metal fire escape steps went straight into the car park and a black Citroën C4, parked on its own. They ran down the stairs and Neil found the door open, a two-door sports version. Neil pulled the seats forward and pushed Irina in the back. He joined her and they stayed below the window level. The next thing they heard was another door opening and David's voice saying "C'est OK, laissez-les tranquilles jusqu'à ce que je revienne. Ils n'ont pas faim et il ya de l'eau dans la chambre. Ne pas les déranger, je veux les faire transpirer. (It is OK; just leave them alone until I return. They are not hungry and there is water in the room. Do not disturb them I want them to sweat.)" David opened the car door, did not look in the back; just fired up the diesel engine and pulled out of the car park.

The car drove through the barrier and into the street, changed lanes and Neil heard his father say, "You two can stop whatever you are doing in the back and sit up now." Neil and Irina pulled themselves up into the back seats and watched as the city passed them by as they swiftly went down streets and were clearly driving out of Paris. Neil had worked this out as they had passed the Air Force Training school buildings with the jet outside on the left hand side of the car. They were going in the direction of Meudon. Neil had read the signs. The car pulled into the car park in front of David's flat. David parked the car and held the door open for the two in the back to get out. "Follow me; we will be safe here for some time." They all went into the flat. David checked the shutters before he turned on the lights. "Old habits die hard "he laughed. "Would you like tea, I have pu-er. It is good for my high blood pressure. David made tea and brought it into the lounge. Neil and Irina were sitting on the sofa and David sat on a straight-backed chair and looked at them both. A nice couple he thought. "OK let's go for your questions and I will do my best to answer them all," said David. Neil started with, "Does anyone know that you are alive in our family? "No." "Does anyone need to know you are alive?" "No." "Are you really committed to the Network?" "No." "Are you married again?" "No, yes!" "Do you have someone in tow?" "No." "Do you say anything other than no?" "Yes." Neil burst out with "Jesus Christ you really are a pain in the arse David." "I would think Neil that you could address me as Dad please." "Why should I, you were never around and never cared for me when I was growing up. You did not leave mum money or send me anything." "None of that is true Neil, 5 years of presents via a solicitor and no response. I paid maintenance on you until you left school at 18. Then, if I remember it correctly your mother sent you back to school and tried to carry on claiming money for you, yes?" Irina felt very uncomfortable at this exchange. "I need the toilet please" "Down the hall and straight in front of you there is no lock on the door." Irina stood up, turned and went through the door into the hallway away from the lounge and the entry to the apartment. She closed the door behind her. Neil turned on his father with years of venom and pain, "You bastard, you two bit bastard. All that time, all that upset, even Uncle Jeffrey did not know. I did not know; everyone kept telling me you were the best NATO intelligence officer in Europe. I lived in your bloody shadow and you were not dead. I ... I cannot believe you are that much of a sick bastard! I bet you have been shacked up with some tart here and having the time of your life." David allowed his son to sound off, did not move, speak, and attempt to stop his outburst in any way. Much of what he was saying was, of course, true. He had found comfort and physical touch with some attractive and not so attractive women on the way. Yes he had lived in France and made certain that no one could find him, if anyone had come looking. No one had. David had not contacted anyone in his family. He mused that he did not know if his brother was still alive or his children. He sent neither cards nor presents now to anyone. No one in Russia, Ukraine, Europe or the UK, David could never really include the UK as being part of the EU. He reflected upon the many years of travelling, the countries and the people he had known. So many faces, so few names, he had learnt that many years ago. David brought the bone china cup to his lips and drank slowly as his son seemed to run out of steam on his ranting.

"So!" His son almost shouted at him and then went silent. David thought what happens next or is it simply so what? He reflected upon the question and enjoyed the silence for a few moments. He listened to his son breathing and thought back to when Neil was a small child and he would sit and look at him sleeping. He was never going to kill this boy, this man for anyone.

"The decision to join the Network has to be yours Neil." It rests upon your perception and agreement with the argument that the World, in general, and Russia, in particular, needs controlling. The way the Network controlled Western societies. You, of course, may not agree with that last statement Neil. A lot depends upon how you see the political landscape and that of control and responsibility of nations. If you see it at all, then the USA is a spent force and the UK has lived on passed times for so long, China, good old state capitalism is a way forward. I believe that Russia is planning and trying to move forward again as a new type of Soviet Union. Here again you may disagree with me, with the Network, and their backers." David's face was plain, unmoving and did not show any form of feeling or concern. "He is still the best strategist," Neil begrudgingly thought.

"Why should I be interested in politics? I have gotten along without politics for many years quite successfully. I do not see the value of starting now. What do you want me to do?" Neil was still wound up and agitated. "I get paid for the work I do, I defend my country and allow others to defend theirs. I believe in meritocracy and honesty, well almost. I believe that what I do is necessary and helps keep the peace. I see the reports and understand the big picture" "Perhaps not as well as your think Neil" his father replied. "What do you think the impact of a new Russian order would have on the world? Who would go up against them? Not the UK that is for sure; not the USA, so that leaves China. The balance of power would collapse and cause chaos. Can you imagine the impact of a Sino-Soviet conflict? Can you?" Neil went quiet and thought for a moment. What would it mean to the West? He had good friends in Russia, as well as the friends that he had in China. No there would never be another world war and not between Russia and the Chinese, or would there? He had that sinking feeling in the pit of this stomach. North Korea possibly, but not China, Russia was not interested in North Korea. What about their nuclear weapons?

At that moment Irina came back and asked, "Should there be a vehicle outside with men getting out of a black Renault van type thing?"

David stood up and said, "No! Go into the bedroom and press the light panel three times quickly Neil and leave immediately. No buts just do it and don't worry about me." At that moment a stun grenade when off and the door flew open, a masked man holding a handgun entered and starting shooting. No discussion, no introduction, just shots. He saw his father move into the line of fire and take three bullets before he went down. Neil turned and pulled Irina into the hallway and moved quickly to the bedroom. He slammed the door shut and touched the light switch. Steel shutters came up and sealed the room as a passage opened up in the floor. Neil looked back once more and saw his father in his mind's eye. Saw his father dying from simple plain gunshot wounds. Having no weapon to defend himself, no chance to negotiate, nothing but the chance to save his son, His only son who had just found him after so many years apart. Neil then went into work mode and took Irina by the hand, gently, but with a degree of firmness so that she followed him down the steps into an underground cellar cum car park. Another Citroen C4 sports parked in an underground garage. Neil opened the door and found a note on the dashboard and the keys in the ignition. The doorway above them had closed and the room above was lost to them. Neil got in and Irina sat in the passenger seat, Neil read the note. "Dear son, if you are reading this note, my plan has failed and number three has taken me out of the equation. As I write this note, I do not know how much I will have been able to tell you and how much you believe my words. This is a special model, well protected; so, you do not need to read the manual.

It is voice activated to your voice and mine alone. When you are free, you can set it up from anyone you wish to in addition to you. Only a total of three voices at one time. Please delete mine, as I will not be able to use it again. You are in no danger reading this note and taking time to prepare for your exit. This cave is a safe house in itself. I suggest you go south to Saumur and use my old apartment. No one knows of its existence. Not by anyone in the Network so you will have time to set up what you wish to do in terms of the Network, the service and the threats that still face you. Your life is still in grave danger Neil. It will remain so until you can take out the late major general. You may feel that going after number three is important. But not important enough to allow number one to run the set-up and attack Russia." Neil sat and looked at the letter and then surveyed the surroundings. He had heard of his father living in Saumur, but did not realise that it was true. He turned the ignition key and a sat nav was set to Place St Michel in Saumur. He put the car in gear and was not certain where they would go, as there was no apparent doorway. As he slowly lifted the clutch, the door opened up at the back of the house and on the road down to the town train station. He drove out and the wall closed and looked like the building again. Neil could hear a variety of noises and shooting going off above them and behind the building. He moved the accelerator down and the car pulled away smoothly and quickly. Soon they were moving down a side street, steep, but easily handled by the car. It stuck to the road like glue and its handling was superb. His father has a good choice in motor cars. He corrected himself; his dead father had a good choice in motor cars. His father was dead. He had seen it happen. He wondered what he would say to his Uncle when he saw him next; would anyone believe him if he told them about his father and the Network?

Neil suddenly did a U-turn. His father was a past master at dying and resurrection. He drove the car at speed in the direction he had come from and came into Meudon from a different angle not from the main square. He slowed down and drove passed the police station as if he was looking for somewhere. It had taken him very few minutes to get away and then return to the scene. Police, a blood wagon and many people were milling around. He drove passed the small park area and turned left. He parked and got out of the car. He turned to Irina and said, "Stay put"! He walked along the road, passed the florist, stood by the railings, and watched the apartment entrance. The front door was wide open as if a gas explosion had occurred with bits of brick, glass and blood everywhere. Neil strained to see if anyone was in the blood wagon. Then he saw that there was a trolley with a body covered by a sheet. A shortish young woman pushed through the crowd and ran to the trolley. She had tears flowing down her cheeks and mascara in long black streaks on her face, a roundish face, full lips and a full figure, running at the trolley; before anyone could stop her she had pulled off the sheet and was kissing the body of his father. The face was relaxed and white; Neil felt that the body was cold. He remembered his father telling him that when his grandfather had died he, his father, had stood outside with his grandfather so that he was not alone. Neil wanted to walk over and be next to the body of his father. He knew that he could not. He could not stand by his dad and not allow him to be on his own. Neil suddenly thought that there were enough chemicals to create a look of death without dead being present. He looked hard at the body, the woman crying, had left the sheet pulled back. He could not be sure, nor could he really believe that his father was now dead. A gendarme asked him to move along and Neil moved away. He knew, really he knew that Major (Retired) David Taylor, his long lost father, was dead. He walked back to the car and noticed that it was empty. He looked about and saw Irina standing a little way away from the car, she was sobbing and her shoulders were going up and down as she tried to control herself. "Get in the car please Irina" Neil asked her. He sat in the car and found that as he was fingering the armrest it came away to reveal a panel of switches and buttons. He looked at the little labels and saw a label video. He pushed the button and then looked up as Irina got back into the car. Nothing had seemed to happen until a screen came down from the car roof and Neil watched a recording of the last few moments of his father's life. The video link had been running and transmitted to some sort of buffer system, so that he could see it now. He watched himself and Irina go into the garage and then the screen split into two. One with him and Irina and the other the inside of the apartment. The man he had seen in Kiev, number three, had come into the room after the man dressed in black had entered and shot a burst of bullets into the room. His father went down, hit in the chest and the left leg. He started to fall and the man in black fired again. Neil could see clearly on the screen that his father had lifted his trouser leg, right leg and pulled a gun out. He shot at the man dressed in black, then his father saw number three and Neil heard the dialogue as his father called the man a coward and a turncoat. Number three lifted his Glock and fired into his father's head three shots and the body fell back onto the futon. Blood coming from the mouth and the hole in the forehead was seeping. The third bullet appeared to have hit him in the chest. Number three walked up and spoke to his father in his last moments of life. "You would never have killed that boy, you are the turn coat. At least this mess makes me number two and the late general will be pleased. He never liked your background and relationships with woman. Well what would you expect from a gay man with a number two who spent most of his time chasing to get inside a woman's underwear." Number three fired the remaining bullets from his clip into the body, into the chest and laughed as the body jumped with the force of the bullets entering it. Neil had said nothing until now, when he turned the ignition and said, "He is a dead man as is the late general. If I have to I will take over the Network and the people at the top now will follow my father. Into hell I hope."

Time to Regroup and then go Home to Kill People

Chapter 11

Neil drove the car onto the motorway the A11 and headed towards Chartres, passed it on his right hand side he kept driving and aimed for Le Mans. He was tired but just kept driving until he had passed Le Mans and turned on to the motorway towards Saumur. He had not passed the horse yet, so he moved the car over and turned into a service station. He got out and walked to the coffee shop. Irina had joined him and he pushed the door lock from the key fob. The car was immobilised. He was not worried or interested in anyone coming after him, the power and the fight had changed. He was no longer the hunted. He was the hunter and people would and will pay for their actions and behaviour and number three and number one would die; of that there was no doubt. He ordered coffee, an espresso and turned to Irina, who asked for a latte. He paid and stood by the high table watching the door. *"Old habits die hard,"* he thought to himself. That was just what his father had said. Irina had said so little since the affair in Paris; she had slept in the car and was much more rested than Neil was. Neil allowed his coffee to cool, threw it down his neck and was striding to the doorway before Irina realised what was happening. She looked like a lost soul running after Neil as he strode to the car. He started the engine, shook his head and said, "Next stop the apartment in Place St Michel, Saumur Irina OK?" "Yes" was the weak reply, He wondered what she was thinking about and why she was not talking. He did not allow her time to settle, in case she tried to make a call or get in touch with the Network. He had not forgotten the betrayal. "Neil I need the toilet please." "Only if I come with you and check," Neil replied. She agreed and Neil entered the women's toilet as if he should be there. Irina closed the cubicle door and wondered if she dare try to ring the Network. Neil shouted for her to hurry up. She put the mobile back in her bag. She had not even thought about a text message. The doors for escape were closing for Irina and she knew it.

Back in the car, Neil remembered the horse statue outside of the city from a job some years ago. He had no real idea that his father had any links with this city. He punched in Place St Michel into the Satnav and saw the road to follow alongside of the river. He drove past the railway station and across the river and then turned left on to the road beside the river, slowed down and looked for the square. He saw a gap and a café on the corner so he indicated and moved into the square. Number one was on his right and the first entry door in the square. He parked the car and got out seemingly not worried about Irina. She tripped along behind him. He locked the car and used the key from the passenger glove compartment to open the front door of the apartment. It was old, above him and to the left was the chateau. Funny it looked somewhat like the Disney castle. Why he wondered? He reflected on how easy it was to use the péage in France. There was a stairway in front and a room off to the right hand side. He walked up the stairs and called for Irina to shut the door and follow. The stairs listed to one side, were old and well worn. He turned the corner and saw the door on the left at the landing one more flight up. He used the keys and the door opened easily. He moved across, pulled the drapes, and then put the light on. Funny there was a straight run to the windows, no furniture in the way. He turned around and saw a lounge and a kitchenette off to the left and a small corridor to the bedroom and the bathroom room. Nice and compact; big casement windows and thick drapes, leather furniture and a computer on a desk against the wall; a few well-chosen books, a telephone, and a television on a chest of drawers. Neil suddenly felt too tired for anything. "I am cleaning my teeth and sleeping" he said and locked the front door using the keypad. "We will have to share Irina, OK?" She nodded and went towards the bathroom. It was small and contained a bath as well as a shower and washbasin. Neil cleaned his teeth using the new toothbrush from the medicine cabinet. He used the toilet and washed himself; then turned and walked into the bedroom. As the curtains were shut, he switched on the light. "Which side of the bed window or door?" he asked. Irina went to the window side and Neil undressed and got into the bed. A firm mattress and the frame did not creek. He was asleep before Irina put out the light and walked around the bed to the window side. She too fell asleep and found herself close to Neil, snuggled in, when she awoke in the morning. Neil had not moved or stirred all night. Irina got up, went into the kitchenette, and put the machine on to make coffee. A Nesperesso machine with good coffee, she waited as the small coffee bowls filled with coffee and the aroma went through the apartment. She felt as if someone was standing next to her. However, when she turned no one was there. On the other hand, was there a shadow of an old man? She could not be sure, but it looked like the shadow of David. It frightened her. She looked about and no one was in the room. She picked up the two coffee bowls and went back to the bedroom. Neil had not moved. He looked peaceful and calm; considering all that had gone on over the past few days. She felt safer with him around. She also wondered what he would do now that his father was gone and he was still a hunted man. At the aroma of the coffee, Neil moved and started to wake up. He lifted himself up, put the pillow on the headboard, and sat up. He drank the coffee greedily and looked at Irina lying next to him. He wanted to say something; but was lost for words and just did not know what to say to her. So he said, "Thank you for the coffee, it was just what I needed." She looked at him and ran her fingers through his hair. He gently took her fingers and kissed them. Then in a flash was out of bed and in two steps was in the bathroom. He slept with nothing on and last night was no exception. He showered and then shaved, lastly cleaned his teeth before he emerged into the apartment and dressed slowly before he asked for another coffee. He sat at the table and looked out of the window at the river. It was flowing steadily and silently and that his Neil thought about his next moves, to kill the late major general and the new number two. He was going to make them pay, and pay they would. He was now in planning mode as he watched the river and made his plans. He reasoned that the Network's order was you took the place of the person you took out. That meant he would go for the late major general first and then take out the old number three who was now basking in the glory of being number two. Not the way his father had said. He would take number one first. The small problem was he did not know who the late major general was. He was going to find out and kill him. Perhaps it was she. Either way they were dead. They just did not know it yet.

  He drank his coffee and thought about his dad, gone at last at rest. How many times had his father's claim to fame was that he had written as a strategist the third world war? His mother had said 26 times. Neil did not know. The man he had never got to know and had only his mother's opinion rather than his own. Well he had style. This apartment was good and the place in Meudon was good too. He had a good coffee machine and a firm bed. So he could not be all-bad, could he? Neil looked out of the window and wondered where Irina was. He stopped, listened, and heard her in the bathroom, in the shower. He visualised her naked body and the water running down it. Then he returned to his thoughts about getting back into England and killing the late major general. They would drive back and come in through one of the quieter ports and then carry on to London. He stopped and though about the fact that he had used the term they. Yes, he would keep Irina close, just in case, just in case. He heard the shower stop and imagined her nipping across the gap and into the bedroom to get dressed. Neil looked out of the window at nothing. The he saw his father's face in front of him. He looking cold, exactly how he had looked on the trolley as they brought him out of the apartment in Meudon. A tear rolled down his cheek and he wiped his cheek and starred. Many years ago, Neil had taught himself to pull the trigger and not to think first. Most shooters did something, a twitch, a deep breath, a moment of decision and that was how you died. He would shoot the late general and then think about it. He would take over the Network and that was a certainty. He knew what he needed to do, yes drive to London and then see the window cleaner first. Then he went into the office and all hell would break loose. Irina waked into the room and looked good, relaxed, beautiful and sexy. Neil had other things on his mind. "Come on" he said, "We are going to see the window cleaner." "Who?" "No, not the Who, the window cleaner"! "OK, I have no idea what you are talking about but let's go." Neil checked the passports for them both, took some money from the draw that was under the TV. He picked up a clean toothbrush from the bathroom cabinet, then remembered that there were two and picked up another. He closed the door and went down the stairs after Irina. He stopped her opening the door and did that himself. No one about, it was the second day since they had arrived and no one was paying them any attention. The café was open and he walked across and took two bottles of water from the stand, paid and left. In that time he looked around and was satisfied that, no one was near the car. He used the remote to open the doors before they got close. No explosion, nothing just the way it should be for a couple getting into their car after an assignation. Irina sat down and then brought her legs into the car, yes good legs, and sexy legs. Sometime soon, Neil thought to himself, if she was willing. He turned the car and aimed for the bridge and out of town to the péage, north and eventually London. He put a disc into the player and listened to Sammy Price, light jazz. He did not feel like that. He ejected it and put on some rock music, Quo or Whitesnake would do.

As the music played Neil thought through the journey, up to Le Mans, turn right, past Le Mans turn left and up to the coast. Then the A3 up to London, stop off for the window cleaner and then go to east London for a meeting with the watchmaker. The window cleaner knew everything that was happening in the capital. The watchmaker supplied weapons like no one else. Neil knew that this time weapons were a necessity, not just talk nor his hands or quick reactions. He meant to kill at least two men. Oh, he thought what if the late major general was a woman. It did not matter he would kill the person and number three. This was personal, as personal as it gets. He looked across at Irina and she had fallen asleep in the car seat, head leaning forward a little. Her hair was over her face and he looked back at the road. How many times his father had driven this route, he wondered. He found himself thinking about the one main memory he had of his father. Neil had been about seven and his father had come into his bedroom and sat on his bed. His father had thought he was asleep, but he was not. His father had spoken quietly to him and told that he would always be there for him not matter what. He had to ask that was all. Neil had never asked, ever. So did that explain why his father was never there? He did not know and now he would never find out. He pulled into the services just past Le Mans and just before the turn off to the coast. He shook Irina and said, "Coffee love?" They walked into the services and Neil went to the toilet first. Then ordered two coffees and stood at a high table to drink his. He needed to stretch and so he walked a little way around the services. Irina had decided not to call the Network, because she felt safe again with Neil. He called Irina and walked back towards the car. He checked the fuel gauge and decided that he could reach the coast before he needed fuel. He started the engine and pulled out into the traffic flow, almost immediately he needed to turn off the péage and take the road north. Irina went back to sleep and he kept on driving, no music this time, just road and thoughts, thoughts and the road. He was thinking what weapons he needed. Would the window cleaner really know who the late major general was? He needed that last piece of the puzzle badly. Was it the last piece? Yes it was! Killing people was not difficult for a man who earned his living by undertaking this type of work. This was his job and he was good at it, very good at it. These two people were as good as dead and no one person was going to stop him. They had conspired to kill his father, because his father had tried to be there for him. Perhaps his father had loved him and his mother was wrong, perhaps?

 Neil concentrated on the road as it was getting dark and traffic was getting worse. He wondered if anyone really did know where he was and what he was planning. Where the Network able to work things out in that detail? They did not have it right so far. The Network had failed to kill him and had managed to upset him to the point where he was going after them. He moved out into the fast lane and put his foot to the floor. Bored with driving in traffic, he wanted to be at the port. He drove steadily at a speed most people would not consider in the light and conditions. It had started raining as he had come closer to the coast, heavy rain and dark clouds and water on the road. The Citroen was up to the task and Neil felt safe in the car as he scanned the road ahead for police or speed cameras. Irina woke up with a start and asked him where they were? Neil replied, "In the Citroen going to the port." She laughed a little and told him he was an arse. Neil smiled and carried on at break neck speed. He had lost the desire to drive and wanted the bedroom on board ship for the crossing. Neil had been driving for some three and one half hours as he pulled into the port entrance and pulled down the window. He explained to the on duty staff who he was and took two tickets and a first class berth voucher. They boarded last and when the doors of the ship had closed, he allowed himself to relax just a little, as he had not checked the room or toured the ship yet. Irina and he went up in the lift and where met by a junior maritime officer who escorted them to the suite. He opened the door and Neil went in last. He passed the man some money and said "no visitors at all." The man nodded and closed the door behind them. Neil locked the door and checked the pictures and lamps for microphones or anything that did not look right. Afterwards he sat down in an armchair and pushed off his hand made shoes. "Do you want to go to the restaurant for dinner or we can have it here?"

Things that do Not go bump in the night

Chapter 12

Neil had ordered steak frites, "a point," with salad. Irina had duck with orange sauce. Nothing seemed out of place. Neil was uncomfortable, very uncomfortable. Neil never liked things that went too well or even exactly according to plan. The road journey was too easy and he had become uncomfortable as he boarded the ship. He had thought and thought about where an attack would come from. From off the ship was not usual, inside the ship meant through the bulkhead or the door. He could not hear any drilling sounds or even tapping, all he could hear was the rumbling of the engines. Then they stopped. Something was wrong; he heard the foghorn sounding in accordance with rule 27, continuously. Irina jumped up and called for a life vest, Neil sat still. This was no easy ship to sink or cause distress. This was a fully loaded cross channel ferry. Neil stayed still. Irina started to run about and shout at Neil. Neil sat still, all he did was to feel inside his jacket and withdraw a 44 Magnum, with a short barrel. Holding the gun in his right hand, he let it rest on his lap. Irina screamed and sat down! "If only that bloody horn would stop," Neil said aloud, but to no one in particular. At that moment, the door burst open. Neil had shot the first person through the door. The junior maritime officer fell, without the chance to cry out. Pushed out of the way by two men dressed in black with balaclavas over their head. The first man seems to be suffering from red coming out of his head and his balaclava. Neil had shot him through the head. Two down in the space of less than one minute. As the third man searched for cover, Neil shot him in the side of his head and the bullet had maximum effect as the gun had the title of a "man stopper." The man sank to his knees as the blood poured from his wound in his head. Neil had not even moved from his seated position. Then he heard a whooshing sound and shouted for Irina to "get down!" A rocket-propelled grenade flew past them and exploded in the second room, the bedroom. The blast went above them, just. Neil was getting more and more pissed off. That was the only term he felt like using. He waited, lying flat on the floor, and after what seemed like an age, a short, stocky man walked down the corridor towards what was left of the suite. He had an RPG in his hand and held it as he died. That was Neil's fourth bullet. He got up, brushed himself down, and then helped Irina up. Visibly shaken, she was trembling. He did not put his free arm around her; just held the gun in a position to use it once more. The foghorn stopped as quickly as it had started and then crewmembers came running, making noise and shouting as they ran. Neil lowered the gun, pulled his jacket on and placed the gun back into the holster inside of the jacket. The first senior officer came in shouting "what the hell!" Neil said nothing and did nothing, which upset the man even more. Neil put his hand up and stopped the man talking Margaret Thatcher style. He shut up in amazement. "This cabin is well below par old man, please arrange from my partner and I to be moved to the captain's berth please and tell him I have requested this." "And who the hell are you?" Neil produced a plain white card and said slowly and deliberately, "give this to the captain; he will understand." The man looked at the plastic card and turned it over in his hands. It was blank nothing on it at all. "Is this a joke?" "Do it" Neil, said, "Do it now!" Neil took Irina's arm and casually walked out of the wrecked cabin and towards the ships bridge. The senior officer in tow, muttering and complaining that he did not know what was happening. Of course, he did not know what was going on and never really would. Seated in the captain's suite, Neil took a drink of hot chocolate. He heard a knock on the door and his hand went into the inside of his jacket. The captain opened the door and came in as if he owned the place, which of course, he did. "I might have known it would be you Neil. How are you these days? Still killing people, I see. But rather more quickly that I seem to remember." "Very sorry about the mess and yes it was quick; but it needed to be! How quickly can you get this tub to port in the UK please? "I will be docking her in about 50 minutes or so and you will leave first. Can you get out if I clear the way through the customs for you?" Neil turned to him and said, "I need you to take care of Irina please. Will you do that for me? She is in real danger." Irina looked at Neil and then at the captain, "You two know each other, how?" "Alan and I were at school together, he was head of Somerset house. I was his number 2. We go back a long, long way; don't we Alan?" "Yes we do and yes I will; come with me please young lady." Irina walked out of the door and Neil did not know that it was the last time he would see her alive. Neil sat down and continued drinking his chocolate; having first removed his jacket and placed it on the chair beside him. He must have dropped into a fitful sleep. He woke to the sound of the ship bumping into the dockside and someone knocking on the door. Neil got up and put his jacket on. He moved calmly to his car and opened the door after he had checked the sills and the boot. He unlocked the car door having stood back and used the remote key fob. The car powered up and he aimed it to go down the ramp.

Neil's head was doing the aircrew thing when flying; rotating their heads all over the place looking in case, they were bounced. He drove down the ramp in a controlled manner, rotating his head until he got out into the early morning light. He quickly; but safely drove through the dockyard and was waved through customs by the uniformed official saluting him. Neil could have done without that. As he reached the roundabout to leave the port, he saw a man levelling a handgun towards him. So that was why the salute. It was to target him. He accelerated the car and drove at the man. God this was getting boring. Normally he would have looked for another way out. No now, he hit the man full on and watched as he bounced off the bonnet and fell to the right of the car as the handgun flew to the left. Neil kept going. Next, stop the window cleaner. Neil took the M27 and drove towards Pangbourne and Reading. He did not worry about this drive as he was going off the track that anyone would imagine. He pulled off and turned for Tilehurst. He pulled up in a close, at a house with plain doors and the front room that did not have curtains. It did have clean windows. He looked into the house and saw the window cleaner sitting on a sofa. Neil locked the car and walked up to the door. A very attractive, but hung over girl answered the door. Before he could say anything, he heard the voice shout out, "Let him in, let the bastard in." "Thank you window cleaner" said Neil. Neil walked into the front room; the lounge and the window cleaner looked up and smiled. He was tall, over six foot, slim, bony and with big ears. In front of him were a variety of TV screens and a radio on in the background. Neil heard a police transmission in the noise somewhere. "What can I do for the UK's most wanted man?" the window cleaner asked. "Jesus you have kicked up a few stones. Please to see you anyway Neil Tea, coffee? Mind you I do not believe a word of it; but the fuzz, were around just in case. I will ring the fuzz 30 minutes after you leave OK. Have to keep on their good side you know. The festival is coming up soon and I do not want them spending too much time with me. OK Neil to business; what do you want from me?" "I need to know who the late major general is." "Phew, tough one Neil; you don't go for easy ones like who will win the FA cup next season." Slight problem the real late major general was your father David. He reported to someone else who was a real Network's major general. Word has it they have just retired from SIS." "Now we are getting somewhere. I guessed that, now who is he or she? How did you know about the Network" The window cleaner did not answer that question, looked at the window and said slowly, "How good is a man with a limp and a Micro-Tavor, with a Kimber Mepro reflex sight, don't think he has plastic tipped bullets. Please don't try and shoot through the window. He will never get through the plating and neither will you!" "Can I transmit through it?" "Of course" Neil used his key fob and flicked the switch as the man, who he could see in the mirror above the window cleaner's fire place. The door mirrors moved out and extended at precisely the moment the man was going to shoot. The shot went somewhere; but, not where he had intended. He limped away as quickly as he could try to conceal the weapon under his coat. This was getting silly Neil thought to himself.

"Come on Window cleaner; give me the detail so I can get out of here" "The last head was Ethel Steiff like the bear. Now get out please and be careful if you use that car!" Neil walked to the telephone box on the corner and rang for a taxi. The cab took him to Whitchurch and he opened a garage in garden of a friend's house just before the estate at the end of the road. He drove the car out. It was dusty, but in good nick for an old car, an old ford Cortina. He travelled down Hardwick Road turned left and drove across the bridge and headed for Reading. He continued to drive to the railway station, parked the car and paid for a ticket. He quickly walked up the stairs to the London platform and was in Paddington in 30 minutes, next the underground to Stratford and the watch maker. It was late in the afternoon when Neil walked into the pawn shop in the shopping precinct. The doorbell rattled as he entered and the watchmaker looked up. "Please put the closed sign up Neil." The watchmaker looked older than Neil remembered. His face was still gaunt and his bones showed through much of his skin. "You ill?" Neil looked hard at the old man; he had known his father well, so he had been told. "You know my dad was not dead, until Paris?" The watch maker did not look up he walked away towards a steel grey door and replied as if an afterthought. "I heard. Your father was a good man and a good friend to me. I for one am sorry to see him go. Are you shopping for revenge; if so I can help? If you are shopping I am out of the business these days. Which is it please Neil?" Neil walked slowly behind the watchmaker and equally dead pan replied, "Revenge the two of them will pay the man and the woman. You knew and you never told me. You bastard, watchmaker; you let me think I was alone and he was still alive. "You knew and you" Neil's voice just stopped.

 Neil placed his mobile telephones in the Faraday cage and walked into the larger room. The watchmaker stopped dead. "Your dad had a pacemaker, no one knew, nearly killed him coming in here. You have a pacemaker?" "No, not yet" Neil replied. "No tracking device will work in here so you are totally safe for as long as you need to stop. Now let us talk some business. What can I do for you son of my godson?" Shocked, Neil had never known. He did not have a godfather; his mother had said it was all rubbish religious stuff. "So you knew dad from the start so to speak?" "I was your father's godfather, and his first referee in the game. Canny operator your dad; as I told the security chap;

if he did not want you to know you will never know. That was your dad through and through. As tight lipped as a virgin is on a rugby boys night out. When he wanted to be. You know Neil you dad only told people what he wanted them to hear. That is why he was so good at what he did. Some say he was the best; much better than that number one woman. But she used him and abused him if the truth be known." Neil looked away at the comment "He was." His father was dead, no escaping that this time and they were going to pay. Pay with interest! Did the watchmaker's comments make sense of the Russia saying the late major general does not wear loafers? He had referred to her. Neil turned to the watchmaker and said, "I need something with a short range, no recoil, not much sound, if any, and is necessary untraceable. By the way what is your name; dad knew!" "If you and I live through this one, I will tell you; at present let us just leave it as the watchmaker for now please. How about something in plastic, coloured if you like! It has no real sound, a slight swoosh and a calibre that will kill at up to 12 feet?" "Yes, in my dreams, I want something now Watchmaker," he said the man's title with feeling and stress that was not lost on the man sitting in a chair in front of Neil. The old man pulled open a draw and threw a plastic matchbox at him. "Oh ye of little faith just like your dad. Open it up carefully and I will dig out some shells, sixteen do you; or are you as good as your father said you are? You will need to get used to it and I imagine a rest in safe conditions. No internet, no phones, just food, good mattress and peace and quiet." Neil saw what looked like a thumbprint on the side of the box. Neil placed his right thumbprint on the mark and immediately a draw came out and then a barrel flicked into place. The watchmaker said, "The thumbprint is the trigger when the weapon is open. Here are the shells. You will need to practice, as it is a little different. It is all plastic. The shells are a plastic and an explosive mix. They are very effective at short range, say up to three feet." "May I try it please?" "Yes, the range is still inside the cage so help yourself I will see you in the morning Neil. Good night and sleep well."

Neil bid the watchmaker a good night and turned to the plastic gun. He walked to the indoor range and put the shells into the back of the weapon. He turned and switched the lights on in the range and saw a target some five feet away. He used the string attachment to bring it closer and then looked to see if the card target was about three feet away. He looked at the weapon again and pointing the barrel towards the target, he placed his right thumb on the thumbprint. There was no shudder no recoil, just a slight hiss of sound and a plastic shell hit the target exactly where Neil had aimed it. He was not only a little surprised; but also very pleased. This would do very well. He tried a few more shots and then switched off the lights and walked back to the table and chairs. On the right hand, side of the room was a bed of sorts with blankets and a thin mattress. He suddenly realised that he was tired again and moved over and switched the small table lamp on it hand a faun coloured shade, which was not round or the usual shape smaller at the top and larger at the bottom. It was more like a cylinder. Neil fell on to the bed and was sound asleep as his head touched the pillow. He slept deeply and soundly knowing that he was safe for the first time in many a night's sleep. Things were not going to go bump tonight. He slept!

Death was Coming, but to Whom?

Chapter 13

Alan opened the door of the sports car and waited for Irina to slide in, knees together and her cute behind moved over the leather of the seat. He jumped into the driver's seat and turned the ignition on. "Flash car" Irina commented and gave Alan a smile that seemed to fill his world. He liked this girl very much and did not mind if she had been with Neil. He liked her style! He drove out of the port gates and headed for the "open road." Was there anywhere in the UK that was still the open road, he thought to himself. He looked down at Irina's legs and again was smitten. "Are you and Neil an item or is there a chance for anyone else?" Alan had asked without thinking aloud than trying to question her. She replied in a purr "why are you interested? The answer is no! I let him down and he will never forgive me." "That is my boy, a lot like his father. Did you know his father or don't you go back that far?" Irina went quiet and then replied in a single word "briefly."

Alan changed the subject and asked Irina about her background; most of which she declined to answer. Alan thought hard for an angle to "Chat this cutie up." Irina seemed to read his mind and said to him "Let's get a room in a reasonable hotel; I am tired of driving and travelling." Alan could not believe his luck. "Are you sure?" was all he could say. He turned onto a bye pass and checked the sat nav, praying for a small hotel to be nearby. Alan was worried she would change her mind. It had never occurred to him that she would want two bedrooms. It did not matter he was busy looking at the sat nav as the sport car hit a tractor head on. The tractor was a moving bomb and it exploded on impact. This caused the sports car to explode and burn. Neither Alan nor Irina knew anything about their lasts moments as the car erupted into flames and explosions. Number two stood in the field watching his handiwork. He switched off the remote control unit and watched with a degree of pleasure that he had now removed the girl. He really was good at his job and Neil was now the next one on his list. He had a meeting with number one first then no more distractions; kill Neil.

Neil rolled over in bed. He was cold and on his own. He hated sleeping on his own and what made it worse was the single bed. He did not know where the man who had killed his father was. He knew where the late major general was due to be in 24 hours' time. A text message from the window cleaner had alerted him to the fact. He wondered why she was going to her house in South London. She lived on the borders of Greater London and Kent. He rolled over again. He then wondered about Alan and Irina. Oh, they were in bed somewhere having fun. Well he hoped so. Alan was single and Irina was attractive. He could not work out the time and did not want to look at his watch in case he had to get up. He was not relaxed, but something said to him rest a little while longer. He rolled over once more. Coincidently at the same time as Neil was waking up Number one, the late major general, was standing in front of her full-length mirror and looked long and hard at her naked body. She worked out and her buttocks flexed and she smiled at the own rear end. The breasts were still firm and not a great deal of sagging. She had never suckled a baby. She turned towards her king-sized bed and saw the young man from the local pub from last night. He was fit but had not managed to make her climax. She had faked it and he seemed pleased with himself; but she was not. She had wanted some satisfaction and something to take her mind of the pressing problem of number two's son Neil. This brief interlude had done neither. She was frustrated on an emotional and physical level. She looked back to the mirror and wondered if she met Neil, could she turn him using herself. She pondered this thought as she looked at her breasts and her flat tummy. More to the point, where was Neil, has he been taken out? Half of her reports had said he had the other half said he was alive and they had no idea where he was. Even the shooter, who had tried at the window cleaner, in case Neil went there, was not able to add anything other than the window cleaner was safe. The shooter had not seen Neil or anyone who even looked like his pictures. She inadvertently felt her left breast and was sure there was a lump that would need to be checked out eventually. However, the matter of this son of David was of much more important. Well the new number two was adamant that it would be resolved equally soon. She took that with a pitch of salt. She then wondered if Neil would go for her or number two first. She mused and then felt cold. She put on her silk robe and tied it tightly. The boy in her bed moved and she called him in a loud voice and told him to get up and get out in that order, quickly. He raised his head and looked exhausted. He had not performed the way she had wanted. She moved towards the door as he called her name to protest "Patricia, come back to bed with me." She swore at him and pulled the duvet from his body. She thought never judge a book by its cover. This cover was excellent the inside did not match up by a long way. No one in the Network ever called her by her name. She regretted using her own name when they had met last night still, "What is done is done. Get out you failure, get out now!"

The new number two was now arriving on the M4. He had slept well in the back of the estate car. He would drop into a hotel and shower, shave and get ready for the meeting. It was set from midnight at Number one's property on the borders of Kent. "Pull into the Novotel please and drop me here." The driver pulled off the one-way system and stopped the car outside the reception doors. Number two got out and walked to the desk. In perfect French, he asked for his room key and ordered a full English breakfast. He took the plastic key and moved to the lift.

The watchmaker came into the cage and had a breakfast tray in his hands. The tray contained espresso coffee, fruit, and porridge. "This was your father's favourite breakfast before a job. Hope it hits the right spot. What was the weapon like in your hands please?" "Watchmaker, if I come out of this I want to act as your marketing manager to sell this weapon. This weapon is outstanding and it shoots in a straight line. How did you? No, do not answer that I do not want to know. I just need to know that it does what you said it did."

Neil got up and sat down to the tray that the watchmaker had put on the table. Watchmaker went out and allowed Neil to his thoughts, his feelings and his breakfast. Neil sipped his coffee and looked up in surprise when the watchmaking came in and took a small box from a draw and said, almost, absentmindedly, "I have to go out; please look after the shop., The meeting has been set for midnight in Sidcup; she is already at home and not due to go out today. The guards will change over at about 9 pm to night. Oh sorry 21h00. What type of wheels do you want?" "A four wheel drive Jeep please, nothing distinctive except what is under the bonnet please" Neil replied. "Everything is locked up upstairs and there are no callers. So anyone who arrives is not expected, wanted or allowed in; whilst you are here OK?" The watchmaker strode out of the room with a sense of determination that Neil had not seen before. He went back to his breakfast.

The watchmaker walked out of the house from the back door, turned down the alley and was at the local bus stop in no time at all. It took him to the bus station in Stratford, which was the hub for the trains, DLR and the over ground railways. He took the underground train, the central line, changed at White City on to the circle line, and got out at the end of the line. It was Hammersmith station. He came out of the station and took a coffee at the entrance cafe. Whilst he drank his coffee, he seemed to be playing with a white matchbox. No one really looked at him. The watchmaker was a true grey man. He was not dressed in anything that anyone would remember. He had glasses that were clear and used only plain side frames. His hair was clean, but not gelled or cut in any noticeable manner. He was wearing brown trousers and a brown fleece. He fumbled with the matchbox, finished his coffee and then got up and walked to around the block to the Novotel. He walked into the hotel and took the lift to the sixth floor. Walking down the corridor to the left of the lift. Anyone watching him would have expected that he was going to his own room as he moved with such a degree of confidence. His intelligence report was correct. George was remembering everything that David had taught him. He had revenge on his mind. The new number two had killed his godson. George stopped at room 610 and used the skeleton keys to undo the lock. He walked into the room as the man inside turned and said "Who the hell are you?" George shot him with a plastic matchbox. It was not really a matchbox; it was another plastic, non-traceable weapon. One single shot through the centre of number two's forehead and the man sank to the ground, bleeding on the carpet. George moved forward and checked that the pulse was missing. He then checked the door and listened. Nothing heard outside. He went to the desk and picked up the sheet of paper number two had been reading. He had not expected any attack in the Novotel, as it was a known Network location, a safe house of sorts. He took a picture of the paper with his Sony mobile phone. He then walked back, opened the door and strode into the corridor as if he was leaving his room. He closed the door and walked to the lift. Exiting the lift on the ground floor, he walked out of the reception and got into the first taxi. A black cab and he asked for the Army and Navy club in Pall Mall. In the back of the cab, he peeled off a pair of wafer thin latex gloves, rolled them into a ball, and put them in his fleece jacket. The cab drove through the traffic at a reasonable speed and arrived outside the club entrance. He paid the cab off and gave a small tip, and waited until the cab had moved off. He then turned into St James Square walked up and into Jermyn Street. He went up the alley and into Piccadilly. George used his freedom pass and took the Piccadilly line to Holborn and thence to Stratford. His revenge complete he put the gloves into a rubbish bin and touched the plastic box for reassurance.

He re-entered the room where Neil was looking at a schematic of a house in Harland Drive, Sidcup. Neil looked up and said "Everything OK watchmaker?" The watchmaker sat down as if he were tired and looked long and hard at Neil. "You wanted to know my name. Your father was my godson and he knew my name. Your father asked me to give you all the help I could and I have done as much as I can. The new number two is dead; you only have to go for number one. He killed my godson and I was not about to let that go unpunished. If you succeed in killing number one you can call me George, OK Neil?"

Neil stopped what he was doing and looked at this old man. This old man had changed from the man who had let him into the workshop and asked him to put up the closed sign. "You did what?" "I was once a field agent for a short while. Your father taught me everything he knew and it is his knowledge that allowed me to go through the hotel room door and just shoot the man. I suppose it is a little like riding a bike. You never really forget no matter how hard you try. At least I have avenged my godson; who was so good to me throughout my life and supported me on so many things." The watchmaker broke down in tears and sobbed uncontrollably.

Neil got up and placed his hand on the man's shoulder. The watchmaker looked up into Neil's blue eyes and Neil said quietly and with great compassion, "Thank you George. You have done a great service to my father's memory and to me personally. You rest now, lie down and rest." George, the old man, was just that again a tired old man. He fell onto the bed and went into a fitful sleep.

Neil moved back to his schematic. The problem was that the property was in three parts, an old set of offices with a garage attached a main part and the granny flat. He was certain that there was an empty granny flat, did the back garden really overlook the allotments, as shown on the map. He had photos that showed a door into the allotments from the garden. The allotments were beside the railway line that went to London and Charing Cross. The time was now 14h00 and he had to finalise his plan. The last piece of the jigsaw puzzle had now been identified, the last killing and then the review and explanation to the mandarins in London. Neil did not know which was going to worse, some asshole in London or some piece of ass in Sidcup. This looked all too easy on paper. Everything looked too easy on paper! He wrote a note to the watchmaker and picked up some suppliers from the watchmakers armoury. He selected a black harness, four stun grenades, the new Glock that had been so evident when Madame Lan and the others had been killed. Was she dead? He opened another cupboard and selected a full-length leather coat, which allowed him to cover everything he had attached to the black harness. Plain black leather gloves and soft-soled shoes, as he dressed inadvertently touched his jade Buddha. He moved on to the last cupboard and selected a small leather bag, in which he placed the electronics to break into any security system. Finally, he checked that he had everything that he needed or might want. He looked at the old man, at George, and slowly looked around the safe haven he had been in for the past few hours. He may never see this place again. After this, he would attend the funeral and then sort out the mandarins. He would also be number one and he needed to decide what, if anything, he would do about the Network. He walked out of the door and out of the shop, back into the street. The street was quiet and he walked to the station alone, short roads and arrived at the main road to the railway and bus station opposite the police station. The weather was fine and dry, which made a change. No rain and no strong winds. He hoped for such conditions in Sidcup. He crossed the road and walked away from the police station to the shopping centre and then through the shopping centre to the railway station. The over ground to Highbury and Islington and then underground to Kings Cross. The final leg would be to London Bridge and a train to Sidcup station. The interchanges were not difficult. It suddenly occurred to Neil that he had made no plans to get out; yet he had made plans for after the killing. Silly or what? He was using George's freedom pass and then he would not register it on the bus to Harland Drive. The journey was uneventful as the darkness fell and he got closer to the Network meeting at Sidcup. He had left his mobile phone at Georges and had no means of calling for backup. As he got off the bus, he could not believe his eye. His Russian support man was waiting for him at the bus stop. It was Eric from the Russian Section 5. Neil could not help himself, "What the hell are you doing here? Are you here to help, hinder, get in the way or try and kill me?" "Sorry Major Olaf, or whomever you really are," said Eric as he produced a knife. He was about to throw it into Neil's chest as Neil kicked him in the groin and Eric dropped the knife as he grabbed his parts. "You two bit little shit Eric. I suppose you are the mole who has been feeding the Network with my movements." Eric could not talk, as he was in intense pain. Eric had not collapsed and Neil kicked him again, but even harder. Taking out the plastic matchbox Neil stared at it as it launched a shell into Eric's chest, close to the area of his heart. This time he did fall to the ground and a few people waiting at the bus stop looked at him. Neil said offhandedly, "Drunk this early in the evening; it is terrible the way this area is going downhill these days." Neil walked off and down Harland Drive. He walked slowly, but firmly in his footsteps. So Eric had told them that he was coming, that was going to make it interesting, very interesting. He was walking on the right hand side of the road, as his target was the last house on the left. Alternatively, the first house on the left or right dependent upon which way you approached it. He continued walking and crossed the road as if he was going to the old people's home and the hostel. As soon as he was in the dark, he turned left and climbed the fence into the allotments. He could see the gateway into the first house and could see the lights on in the kitchen. A neat and tidy kitchen, which seemed to have every gadget you, could ever want. A couple of servants were moving about and taking trays through the door and into the room on the left of the kitchen. Neil stood still and thought about his approach and the things that he needed to do before he would enter the house. The lights were on in the main bedroom on floor one. As the curtains were open, he could see through the window. Neil could see a woman, naked, and trying to dress by putting different dresses in front of her body. A train went passed and the lights shone onto the allotments. Neil was still in the shadows. No one would see him, unless someone was using a night scope. He looked across the allotments and could not see anyone moving and he opened his mouth and listened. Neil felt a gun pushed into the small of his back as someone whispered in his ear to move slowly forward to the gateway and no funny business. "Shit" said Neil. "No thanks I had one before I came on duty. Jesus you are such an amateur. You were supposed to be good. I would never have caught your father like this Neil. He was a good number two. Was it you took out the new number two, because if so you are number two?" "I want to speak with the late major general?" "She said to send you up after we had searched you. So yes I can agree to that demand." "Will she mind if I smoke?" "What in her bedroom, you can take up some smokes I will give you. I do not have a lighter or matches." They were moving through the gateway and the naked woman had turned to see their progress. "I have matches you can check them when we get in the house, if you wish?" Neil kept his pace slow and steady. "Did you kill number two?" Neil said nothing and the man approached the backdoor, which led into a snooker room beside the kitchen. He guided him around the corner and into a bathroom. "Strip now please, everything, except your match box. Will that cover your modesty?" The man laughed as Neil started to take his clothes off. He was very interested in Neil's body and started to stare as he dropped his trousers. Neil turned away from the man and he sighed slightly. Neil then moved with great speed turning and kicking the man on the side of his head. The gun fell to the floor with a clatter. This still seemed too easy. "Is everything all right." "Yes" said Neil and the man outside the door seemed to stay put from the farting noises coming from the other side of the bathroom door.

Neil came out, naked as the day he had been born in Kings Lynn hospital. The white plastic box firmly held in his cheeks. "Oh I see he managed to dip his wicked. You not that way inclined. Pity he always enjoys a first timer." "Just sore from forced entry and do me a favour just shut up and take me upstairs," said Neil.

Neil arrived at a closed bedroom door. The man knocked and opened the door, but did not try to enter. Neil walked in with a slight attempt to hold his cheeks tightly together. This time the curtains were shut and the light was not bright. On the bed was a very attractive woman wearing a smile. "Got you Neil, more easily than I got your father and more easily than I thought. You did not seem to put up a fight. Please come and sit beside me." She patted the bed next to her and Neil moved over to the bed. He remained standing. She was very attractive and in very good nick for her age. "So you are number one and the retired major general" as he sat on the bed and relaxed his cheeks. It was then that he noticed that he had an erection and could not stop himself. "Patricia laughed and said, "Yes, you are standing up like a soldier, nice to see that you find me of interest. Let's talk Neil and see what we can agree?" She leant forward and rested her breasts against his chest. "Did that brute try and have his way with you? Do you need some cream?" "No, I am fine, just a little sore. I am sure you can do something with your hands to help me out." Patricia laughed aloud and touched his shoulder. Neil put his hand behind his back and she pulled him towards her on the bed. Neil moved as if he was going to get on to the bed. Instead, he picked up the plastic box from where his ass had been. Touched the thumbprint, then repeated the action, and watched as the shells went into her open mouth. He touched the pad once more and put the last shell into her forehead. She fell back mouth still open and lay lifeless and limp. Her body emptied its liquids and Neil moved away from the bed. He touched the plastic box and the barrel returned inside the box. Well the plan had worked, caught, compromised, and kill her. That part had become an easy action. He wondered if he should have taken her offer of sex. He somehow thought that his father had always said no and he felt better that he had not succumbed to her charms. Now what was he going to do?

A meeting in London, A funeral in Paris and a flight to China?

Chapter 14

Neil sat on the edge of the bed, naked and feeling exhausted. "Tension" he said to himself. He had achieved what he set out to do and now instead of laughing, he felt like crying and he did. Large tears rolled down his face and he used the back of his hand to wipe them away. He wondered if his father knew what he and George had done; or was it what George and he had done. Neil had real trouble focusing his mind. He had seen his father killed, nearly been killed himself, learnt from George that the original number three had been killed when he thought he had become number two and was home and safe. Then he, Neil, had killed number one, whilst being naked in her bedroom and with a fast failing erection. He knew that killing made some of the departments operatives get their "rocks off." Not for him and he now felt cold and very, very alone. What should he do now? Before he could consider this, a knock came at the door. "We saw everything on the monitor sir, sorry number one. Would you now like to chair the meeting all of the members have arrived as requested?"

"OK but, get me my clothes and that idiot who brought me in to the house." Neil dressed and then looked at the guard who had been so pleased that he alone had captured Neil. "Well sonny Jim you got that wrong didn't you?" "But I was doing as I was told." "You were not told to try and physically attack me, were you? I will offer you a job in the new Network as my driver. "What is your Name?" "Driver" was the reply. Now go down stairs and tell everyone I will be there is two minutes, no smoking, no drinking and no slopping off!" The newly appointed driver, left the room quickly; but with a degree of quietness that pleased Neil. Strange after all that had occurred he was grateful for the quiet. Oh for a life of peace and quiet. He would be so hacked off with total peace and quiet all the time. He walked out of the door and down the stairs to the lounge. He had his plastic box reloaded and ready just in case. He entered a tastefully decorated room with a large mirror over the fireplace. A log fire was burning brightly in the fireplace. The "members" were seated on the easy chairs and sofas spaced around the edges of the room. The curtains were pulled and no lights could be seen from outside. As Neil entered the room, everyone stood up. No one person was slower than anybody else was. Good sign he thought to himself. "Good evening all, as you know I am the new number one, and was the mark that many of your operatives tried to kill over the last few weeks. You will call me either number one or sir; I will tell you if you are a close enough friend to use my name. I believe that we are here tonight to adjust our constitution. Am I correct?" All the members nodded their heads in approval and agreement. No one seemed to want to challenge him now. "Sit and someone get me an espresso, a double if it can be managed. I manage not by debate, but by decision. I may ask for your comments from time to time. However, the final decision will always be mine. Is that clearly understood?" No one raised a voice, until a tall man with a pin stripped suit raised his bony hand and in a clear voice said, "Why should we accept you as number one. We have no evidence that you removed the late major general; you are no more than a Major Retired. We have always been guided by a senior officer, not by some upstart, with a dubious father." Neil turned to face this man and said in a very severe voice, "And who the hell are you? Alternatively, "on the other hand," have all the social graces gone from this so-called organisation? I at least introduced myself. I know you have all seen the video of me naked and the demise of the naked late major general. Your existing rules say that if a junior kills a senior they adopt that position." "But you were not a Network junior!" "I am, as you will remember that the late number three offered me to join the organisation when I was in Kiev. He never met me to discuss my answer. He was too busy killing my father. So unless you can raise something relevant, shut up! Oh! Who are you and what is your number or position?" The man looked at Neil and replied, "We don't give names only number. I am number seven if that matters to you?" Neil was now tired and fed up with this bunch of has been. "You all sound like a bunch of old freemasons with nothing really to complain about. However, I know you are going to complain. I was taught to be cautious and you had better believe it. Anyone who is not with me is against me. You all remember the video of what happened to Patricia, don't you?" The old man coughed and tried to say something else; then thought better of it. A woman rose to her feet and straightened her dress, not good quality and it had seen better days. She wore open toe sandals and thick brown tights. Neil thought she looked ridiculous. She opened her mouth to speak. The man sitting opposite her in the lounge waved her away. "This is your last chance to declare for me or against me. I will go around the room, your will introduce yourself, by name, and then number and declare for or against. You driver, you will keep the tally. Please remember every one of you. I am number one not a junior upstart. Also I can kill anyone who challenges me."

Neil sat down and pointed the man on his left. A good quality suit, clean shoes, yes the loafers, and a silk tie. He rose, said, "I am Sir Eric Charles, I declare for number one," and promptly sat down again. The next person was the woman with the "passed it sell by date" dress. "I am Ethel Grimshaw and I don't decide for number one." She sat down equally quickly. There was a total of nine members plus Neil, so he was waiting to see what would happen next. The next member was a tall, over six foot, broad shouldered rugby player by his looks and damage to his face and ears. "I am Ian and I declare for number one. We need someone to take charge, otherwise we will not only be disorganised, but also disbanded." He sat down slowly as if he had an injury. The next three also declared for Neil and that meant he needed one more member. The next man was the one who had motioned for Grimshaw to sit down. He rose up slowly and looked at all the members present. "I do not declare for any member and not for number one. In so doing I know that I must take the simple way out. I wish you luck and good judgement young man. If you are half as clever as your father the Network will flourish under your tutelage." At this point he appeared to bite his tongue and feel to the floor. No one moved. He was dead before his body actually hit the dark blue carpet in the lounge. Neil still needed another vote! The next two declared against him and Neil was getting worried, well a little. He fingered the plastic box, but not the thumb panel, yet! A small man with a monocle stood up and said in an excited voice, "Stop this nonsense. Number one is number one by right. He took out Patricia. Good job too is you ask my opinion. I was getting so angry about her affairs and not running the organisation. We should never have agreed to her proposal with the late number three to take out David and Neil. I vote for number one and that casts his number of votes required. This man's father was my friend and I was almost powerless to help him because of that man and woman. He was kind to my wife and me when we were on hard times. He kept us going until my shares produced a large sum of money. He would not take anything from us in return. Only that we remain his friends and that I have done and would do to my death bed; David was a man of honour not someone who climbed upon other's backs to get ahead." He sat down and then remembered that he had not mentioned his name as tears started to roll down his fat cheeks. "I am Alan M, number five. David and I were friends sat school. He even said I was a better swimmer than he was. He was, of course correct, in those days. I am Doctor Alan M to be precise." He sat down in his chair and nodded to Neil.

"The vote is over Madam Grimshaw do you wish to leave as the gentleman did or how would you like to go?" Grimshaw did not answer in all the fuss of Alan M she had bitten the poison capsule in her mouth and died in her chair. "Driver get rid of the bodies and start to tidy this place up. I have to leave for London and a meeting with a few mandarin's later this morning. Is there any more business for the moment?" A silence had covered the room and Neil got up and left by the front door having walked out of the lounge without looking back. He sighed a deep and long sigh as he walked across the forecourt and saw that the driver had a dark car ready for him. Neil could not decide the make. "No, this one will not do Driver." As the driver slammed the door, close and started to walk away the car exploded into a ball of fire. He still was not safe yet. Neil walked to the end of the road and took the first bus to the railway station. The meeting had not taken much longer than he thought it might take. There were still many questions unanswered. He had told Driver to stay there and he would get in touch if needed. This part of Southern trains did not run a first class service. Neil was happy to sit amongst the workers travelling to London. He sat next to a man wearing overalls and reader a copy of the Sun. Neil did not look over his shoulder to see page three or any other; pages. His mind was set for his next meeting at 8 am at Charing Cross. He left the station and crossed the road, walked up past St Martins and then carried on up past Costa coffee shop crossing the road by the police station and walked into Porky's pantry. Neil sat down in a vacant booth as the café had only just opened. Bacon eggs and a small coffee please Mark. "The best bacon and egg in town" Neil said to no one in particular. He took his time over the breakfast and Mark asked how he was keeping? "Well enough, a few changes; but, we'll enough!" Neil paid and left the café and walked into Trafalgar square. He crossed the road and stood in front of the closed gates to Drummond's bank. The doors were not open, yet. He went to the cash point ATM machine and pressed the keys a voice spoke to him. "Yes?" "Please tell Sir Joseph that I am here and let me in please." He walked back to the door in time to see the door open and a member of the staff unlock the gate. He entered and the man locked the gate again. Once inside the man said, "Have not seen you for many a year Neil. How are you keeping?" "Tell you later and bring you up to date with the news. But at present I am required upstairs." Neil turned left, opened the door, and climbed the stairs to the room with the Adams fireplace. He tapped the door and entered. Sir Joseph was seated. "Sit down Neil. I am pleased to see you all in one piece. There were times when I wondered if you would ever get through this one. Became a blood bath and you were the last man standing. I am sorry for your loss, only knew him when he was going undercover. Just after, I arrived in the department. I retired from the Army. Your father in the Army? I remember he was insubordinate, when I brought the team in for work early, 06h00 and at 08h55 he said he had to go and get his lunch from the NAAFI wagon, and I was ready to start work. No respecter of rank you father Neil. We lost some good people; but, not you." Sir Joseph carried on like this and Neil sat back and looked at this dapper gentleman, silk tie, white cotton shirt, handmade suit and polished, handmade leather shoes, no not loafers. He stopped talking and sipped his Earl Grey tea. Neil could smell the aroma. "My father made substantive major. I expect you made Brigadier Sir Joseph?" "Actually did slightly better than that Neil." He then started again, "Please submit a report sooner rather than later. I have another task for you now! I need you to go to China and make contact with the number one of the Network in Beijing or Wuhan or Qingdao. I don't know where she is." "What no rest and recuperation? When do I go please? I have a funeral to attend in Paris." How did he know about the Network? "Yes I know we will fly you in and out, a few loose ends. I am not very happy with things. Want to take you out of the game. However, I don't want to change all the good work you have achieved?" Neil took a small white plastic box from his pocket and played with it rolling it in between his fingers. He had been deriving a conclusion and decided that two and two really do make five. A retired officer higher than a Brigadier, no loafers, he knew his father. Someone who knew about the Network and what had been happening. Someone who had the authority to make movement decisions. This was number one not Patricia! The quartermaster will meet you and give you all of the paperwork, diplomatic passport and then details for China. You can't take that stuff with you to Paris." Neil looked hard at Sir Joseph and said slowly and deliberately, "How would you know what was happening and who was being cremated in Paris? How would you any of the last day or so, unless you were there? Are you wearing two faces Sir Joseph? Tell me were you in the Int corps by any chance?" "Why do you ask Neil?" Because the woman I killed, last night is not the deceased number one. I think that you are! You are the person who went after my father and sanctioned the Network's number three to kill him. I know you hold a grudge, or else why would you tell me about dad upsetting you. You are an asshole, a liar, a bastard and the man I need to kill" "Don't be ridiculous man. I am your boss." "No, I am sorry to say that you are not my boss any longer. I am correct you are the late major general." Sir Joseph moved uneasily in his chair and somehow he had managed to level a handgun at Neil's chest. "You are as clever as your father said you were. He was right as usual. Did you know that for years he never called a military intelligence situation incorrectly? He knew military intelligence like most people know how to read the newspaper." The gun was still levelled at Neil's chest. Neil smiled and knew that he had taken too long; he played along with this overconfident fool. Neil had not really expected to find number one here. He had expected more fighting and killing in the future. He stood up and looked directly at the man behind the table with a gun. Was he a trained killer or an amateur? A real amateur, Neil placed his thumb on the pad and then again, in an instant Sir Joseph had a neat small hole in his forehead. Blood ran slowly down the man's contorted face and into his mouth. Yes, yesterday had been too easy. Nevertheless, this was unexpected.

He picked up the papers from the table whilst pressing the plastic box once more and the barrel disappeared. He checked the pockets of the dead man and took all the papers and the leather note block with the distinctive paper from Smythson. Neil attached his Mont Blanc biro to the note block and walked out of the office, down the stairs and out of the, now open, Drummond doors. He looked a grey man for the world to see. Funny too early, he thought, and this made him stop at the top of the stairs by the iron gates. This place was very, very open and he suddenly felt exposed and unprotected. He had the plastic box, but no real weapon and it even felt wrong.

A youngish Chinese woman was passing by the bank and Neil Called out to her, "Ni hao!" "(Hello!)" She stopped and this gave Neil his chance. He went straight up to her and explained that he needed help. "May I ask would you walk me to the railway station please? What is your name please?" She retorted sharply, "I am not some kind of call girl you can pick up on a London Street." At the same time that he was thinking about the underground entrance and the girl, he wondered if the tasking was fake, or would the quartermaster make contact. As they reached, the entrance stairs down to the underground a bullet hit the metal plate of the entrance. Neil pushed the woman down the stairs and threw himself after her.

These failed attempts to kill him was becoming a real pain in the ass. He may be the last man standing; but, whomever they were, they were going to try to change that situation. The woman screamed and complained loudly as Neil continued to push her gently down the stairs. Londoners stopped to look at them, but no one tried to help the woman who kept screaming. No, do not take the underground, too enclosed. They walked, well held the woman's arm so she could not run away as they walked across the underground station concourse and up the exit that would bring him to Waterstones and the South African Embassy. Neil felt tired and flat after all that had gone on. He enjoyed his job. Nevertheless, this was not his job; this game is staying alive. A trip to China did sound good, yet many of his friends had been removed for no reasonable reason. He had to sort this mess out. He was walking, thinking and taking the Chinese woman with him. She changed his train of thought when she started screaming abduction. AT which point simply let her go. He was above ground and more concerned with staying in one piece.

Neil walked up towards Charing Cross station and saw the "Big Issue" seller standing still not moving. He waved as he crossed the road. This was not the time to stop and give him some money. He jumped on a 176 going to Penge. Got off at Waterloo, took the underground now to Warren Street, changed for Kings Cross and the Eurostar. He would worry about the quartermaster alter. He would pick up that thread when he got back, if he got back.

He walked through the underground station turned right and up the slope to St Pancras International station. He wanted a coffee, but he bought a first class single and then went back to Costa for a double espresso and ginger biscuits. He walked up to customs and security entrance, showed his ID card as a member of the company and slipped through without any inspection. He hung around until the last minute and then boarded the train. No one had joined the platform after him nor boarded the train. He had a brief two and one half hours respite, as the train had no stops. He used the time to think about his father's funeral. He had booked a solo seat and had no one behind him. So felt able to relax a little and found himself falling into a slumber. The "coffee jockey" served a meal, which he did not eat and declined coffee or anything else, except hot water. He had checked the carriage when he boarded. Deciding that he should check everything once more before he left his seat for the toilet. He thought to himself, *most of the people did not look out of place. No one was too noisy or too quiet. A family with two children, a looker with legs up to her armpits, oh what a sexist comment.* Then he noticed her at the exact moment she noticed him. It was the Chinese woman from Trafalgar Square. She stood up and called the conductor towards her, words like murderer, scoundrel, robber, and kidnapper could all be heard. The train manager turned to her and said in a loud voice, "I'm sorry madam you are mistaken. This man works for the government and is a diplomat. He travels with us on many occasions. Please sit down or I will have to ask you to leave this carriage and accompany me to my office on board." He nodded to

Neil and glared at the woman. She became quiet and said, "Sorry, I must have been mistaken." Neil went to the toilet, washed his face and sat back in his seat. The rest of the journey was uneventful. However, the woman did keep looking at him, as she was not sure what she had been told. On arrival at Gare du Nord Neil telephoned a request for a car to meet him at the side of the station, near the taxi rank, but not with the taxis.

It was early afternoon and the funeral was set for 15h00. He arrived early and checked out the location both inside and out. Neil was amazed at the number of people who were there. He could not see any of David's ex-wives, thank god. People he had never seen or known about before, a good turnout of people from China, Russia, Ukraine, Germany, France, America, Africa, of course England and even some from Malaysia. However, it was the music was what struck him at the service. People all walked in to Edith Piaf song "No regrets," in French. "Sweet Home Alabama" followed that. As the curtains covered the coffin, "Guide me oh They Great Redeemer" was playing using Cum Rhonda as the music. Neil knew that his father had sung this for his father at that funeral. His dad's voice was the only thing that betrayed his Welsh heritage. Neil did not sing, as he had a lump in his throat, at this point. The music to leave was "Chopin's Nocturne in E." The last oration was the quartermaster speaking about his dad. The man everyone else seemed to know and respect and he did not! Neil hung about outside the church until the quartermaster came out. It was as if everyone knew his dad; but most people did not know that he, Neil, was his son. The quartermaster paid his respects and gave him a brown leather "Textier "document case and walked away. He said as he left, "The keys for the apartment in Meudon are in the document case." Then Neil was standing alone and he was not sure what to do next. A small woman coming up to him and said, "Think I am your half-sister." "What the …

Who are you? I don't have a sister, you must be mistaken!" The woman did not move away. She was smartly dressed in classic, little black dress. Chanel Neil wondered as he looked at her. He stood and looked at her hard and realised that she was crying. She was the woman who had been crying at the apartment in Meudon. Then said, "I have had enough surprises for one day. How about some coffee?"

They sat on the terrace of a café and drank coffee together. She recounted a tale that amazed Neil. His father had a serious relationship after his four wives, one that had meant more to him than anything else. Neil said, "How could he have a child; he had the snip? The reversal failed I know I was told." "Yes but your father, my father, our father was a resourceful man and he did a variety of things from Traditional Chinese medicine to taking testosterone tablets daily for many years. Eventually I was born. His Chinese wife was some thirteen years younger than he was. He so wanted their child, he wanted her to have his child and I am the result. I live in Paris and mum lives in Qingdao. She wanted me to give you her address for you to visit please." Neil had forgotten his problems and threats he was learning something about which he had no previous knowledge, his father recent lifetime. He ordered more coffee and the woman started speaking again. "Your, no our father, loved my mother." She took out a small paper and card frame and in it a picture of Neil's father kissing a Chines woman, no a lady. The picture showed a woman with style, class and someone who looked totally committed to his father. They both looked relaxed and deeply in love from the expression on their faces. The waiter brought the coffee and hang around. Neil threw a few notes, some euros, at him and he wandered off. That was enough to bring Neil back to his work, job and his life. He took the piece of paper with the name and address of Mrs Lucy Taylor. "I am so sorry; but I have to catch an airplane and need to get to the airport." He felt for the document case, which he had not even opened. I have to go to the bank and then to his dad's apartment. "Can I give you a lift?" The woman got up to leave and said, "No I live here and I thank you for your kind offer. I know about the place in Meudon." Neil touched her arm and said, "I don't even know your name. I can't spend the rest of our lives calling you sis?" "My name is Kathleen, I believe after your grandmother." Neil rose and kissed her on each cheek; he pushed his contact details into her hands and then left. She hailed a cab and so did he; they went in different directions. Would he see her again? She seemed genuine. The pictures she had shown him would have been difficult to create, really. He asked himself. He would visit Lucy if that was her real name and check her out. He would know if it was a set up.

Neil sat back in the taxi. He had to go via Meudon and pick up his new set of matching Samsonite luggage. Well at least some things never change. The taxi was told to wait and Neil went into the apartment that about a week ago had been the place where his father had died. Neil check if the garage was still in working order. It was! So he walked out paid off the taxi and went back and opened the document case. He was booked on the ten to one night flight from CDG. He read the papers and then burnt them. What was going to happen now? He went into the cellar and into the basement garage. He had carried the luggage with him and he got into the smaller Citroen and activated the garage door, which in turn closed up the apartment. He drove towards CDG. All he knew was that he was number one in the Network; he was still in a job with the UK, French, Ukraine, Chinese, and Russia governments. He was not so sure about the Chinese; but that was where he was heading after London. It started him thinking about the Network, the late major general and he decided to park the car at Gare du Nord and take the train to London instead. He needed to be in Moscow first and he would go via London! That was his next move, breaking the plan again. Neil pulled into the staff car park at Gare du Nord and sat back in the car seat. No one was about that he could see. He sat still and waited, just in case something happened. This time it did not! He had parked next to his "other" car. Suddenly he though I can drive to London. He was changing the plan too many times. He remained in the seat thinking about all the changes that had happened and their outcomes. His mobile rang and he answered it after checking the number. He said nothing and listened to the voice at the end of the phone. "Is that Dr Taylor please, Doctor Neil Taylor?" "Yes" was Neil's curt reply. "Sorry to bother you sir, but we wondered if you were going to come back for the inquest investigation; as you did not arrive at the airport?" Neil yawned and then said very slowly and with his London accent "Who wants to know? If it is important, they can ring me direct. Please pass that on to the mandarin who asked you to ring." "I am sorry to disturb you sir, but Sir Joseph's replacement asked me to ring. He does not know, well, he has not met you for some time. So he thought it better I called you." Neil sat and looked at the blank wall in front of his car; he sighed, shrugged his shoulders and then said, "Please pass me compliments to Sir Joseph's replacement that I would be happy to accept his call, at his earliest convenience. However, I am on my way to London, but uncontactable for a while. By the way who is Sir Joseph's replacement, and whilst I am asking, who the hell are you?" "Me sir? Me sir, I am the under-secretary to …" The voice trailed off as if he was not sure if he should say anymore. "So I can tell the boss you are on your way, may I?" "You can tell your boss whatever, you want Mr Under-secretary. Please tell him that if he is in Sir Joseph's old office I will visit him after the inquest and before I take a well-earned vacation. Will that suffice?" Neil did not wait for an answer he hung up and threw the mobile on the seat next to him. It bounced onto the floor and he did not move to pick it up. He sat and thought again. Who was following him and why had he not spotted them?

Neil looked around the car, using the mirrors and decided that he could vacate and get into the special. The special was a "Land Rover" with bulletproof glass and armoured bodywork. He felt that he needed some safety around him and under him. The special gave one that feeling of security. In fact, a special had saved his life more than once. He picked up the mobile and took out the battery. Picked up his cases and put the mobile and the battery in the smaller of the two. He moved out of the car and checked the Rover by waving his foot under the bottom of the vehicle and the tailgate opened. He stowed the luggage, felt for a gun, and then remembered that he did not need to be in the special. He did not have one with him anyway. Quickly, very quickly he dropped to the floor and checked the underneath of the car. His experienced eye was looking for something attached to the floor of the vehicle. Although it was fitted with a trembler, an activation switch which would sound an alarm if someone or thing attached anything to the bottom of the vehicle. He saw that the small control box was showing a green light. He got up, dusted himself down and jumped into the driver's seat. He shut the door and activated the internal locking system. Nothing could get in unless he released that switch. The leather was comfortable on his back and the seat was designed for him. He suddenly wondered how much the tax payers had paid for the vehicles that he had written off. So far, he had lived a charmed life and he was very, very lucky. His mind was about to drift as he felt safe, when the small video screen caught his attention it was flashing and had been the whole time he had been in the Rover. He pushed the play button and was totally taken back to see his dead father. He turned the volume up and started the video tape clip again.

"Hello son, I thought that at some stage you would use a special and left this message for you in case I had been taken out. Yes, I am gone, for real this time. I had so little time to talk with you and so little time to share anything with you. If you are hearing this clip, you are safe. Wherever I am, I am thinking of you and wondering if you have met your stepsister. Please go and see Gui. You will know her as Lucy. She knows all about you and wants to meet you. I know you will like each other. You need to settle down sometime son. Sorry I am not here to give you advice, just to say I love you and wish you the very best on everything you do. Goodbye Neil, take care my one and only son." This screen went blank and Neil was not sure how are why his father had managed to get into this special. How did he know that Neil would change his mind and go for this vehicle? How could he know? Neil had not even known. Neill saw a shadow go past the window, and he looked up. A small perfectly formed tear was rolling down his left cheek. A single tear, pear shaped and clear. It fell from his face onto his trousers. Neil pulled out the white, Egyptian cotton handkerchief, wiped his cheek, and then blew his nose. It was time to move and not to linger. He could think about what might have been later. He put the key fob into the slot on the dashboard and waited, five seconds later the care started up and the electronics fit came to life. All round surveillance cameras gave him a view of everything around the vehicle. A computer screen was going through system diagnostics and reported a full weapons fit, full tank of petrol and a map set for the whole of Northern Europe, and a communication's panel. The screen then showed him a list of the food on board, the first aid kit contents and the satellite radio frequency codes for the next hour. As he sat in the safety of the vehicle, Neil felt, alone, very alone. He kept feeling like since Tatiana died. Was he getting too old for fieldwork? He had lost his father after having found him, Irina was gone, and he had a sister, well a stepsister and a stepmother. Both of which he had never known. His mother had gone to glory and he had no girlfriend, she had died in Odessa, no wife, nothing and no one, just the job. He had lost his best friend in Kiev, by his own hand, some would argue. All this really did make him reflect upon what he had achieved in his life and what had his father had achieved. Had either of them actually achieved anything? Anything worthwhile? He put the car into gear, reversed from the park slot, and pulled into the Parisian traffic. He headed northeast and the motorway to Calais and the Eurostar terminal.

No, it was not the end, not even almost. Just the depth of the "SH1T" was changing! Not even his habits were changing.

Neil drove the first part of the journey as he enjoyed driving, and the act of missing cars that wanted to cut him up and get in front was fun. It was a little like driving in China, where everyone still drove cars as if they were riding bicycles. This was France and you could almost hear the drive shouting pardon as they cut you up. He was driving up through Picardy. Eventually deciding to use the self-drive and cruise on the special. Well it was the special! The car had sensors on each wing, roof and each bumper. This meant that it could see traffic around itself. In cruise control, it could speed up or slow down as the traffic conditions required. Neil mused to himself, so much for the experimental self-drive cars. The special had been around for some time, but was not for public consumption. It also had a few extras, which made Neil feel safe. Yes, the bulletproof glass windows and shutters that came up at the press of a switch, glass that reacted to the light. They could go black instantly; plus a pair of machine guns in the front and rear of the grills. No cheap ejection seat, this was the real world not James Bond. The door panel contained a Heckler and Koch MP5SD6 with a retractable buttstock; 3-round burst trigger group, and an integrated suppressor. He liked the three round burst. Easy release from its holder in the vehicle and very effective. Still he went back to driving and pushed the buttons to cruise and self-drive. Neil then pushed the seat back and dozed for a short while. Yes, he trusted the car; yet he still trusted his ability more than any machine. Neil must have been asleep as he woke with a start as his private telephone was ringing. "Who the hell is ringing me now?" he said aloud but to no one. He pushed the communications button on the seat and said "Hello."

"Neil? Neil?" it was an old voice and Neil recognised it as his uncle. "Hi there, how are you these days, long time no speak Uncle Jeffrey." "I am sorry to disturb you, can you talk please?" "Yes for you, how can I help?" His uncle was some years older than his father was. He had lived longer than his dad had. Not surprising that they did very different jobs. "I have just received a communication from France saying that your father is dead. He died years ago, can you tell me what is happening," after a pause he said "Please Neil what is happening?"

"Uncle Jeff, I am driving in France at the moment. We need to talk, but now is not a good time. Yes, dad is dead; I attended the funeral in Paris and met my stepsister. When would be a good time for me to ring you back? I really can't talk now." "Whenever you are free, do not worry about the time. I just do not understand. Mind you, with your Dad I never really did understand. He was my brother, yet I never really knew where he was and what he was doing. I knew he was a spy for a while. I even told him so. Sorry Neil I am going on. Ring me when you are free." The phone went dead.

Neil reflected upon the fact that everyone in the family had said Jeffrey would go first. A quadruple bypass, angina, diabetes, and gout. He had outlasted them all. He was a naturalised American and lived in New England, on his own. His wife had passed away a while ago. He was Neil's family, even if they did not talk much.

Switching the car back to normal drive, he turned into the ferry terminal and showed his Pass to the booth operator. She waved him through after a second glance. Another time he thought, another time perhaps. He had business now and business and pleasure do not mix too well. Directed to the front of the train and into a compartment, which was sealed with him in there, on his own. An inspector came up and tapped on the window. Neil did not open the window, but flicked another communication switch and spoke to the man. "Problem?" "No sir, just checking." "Checking what?" Neil asked. "I have never had one of you aboard before. I know the drill I will be about if you need me." "Oh! Thank you chef" Neil replied and switched off the communicator. A short while later the train pulled out and Neil hit the protection switch on the dashboard. The shutters came up, the windows went black and the sensors came up on the screens inside the vehicle. Adjusting his seat, he relaxed, well he thought about relaxing, when he noticed that someone had come into the sealed area and was approaching the car. The man had a silly mask on his face. He was certain that it was a man from the walk. This chap was tall and with big shoulders, an odd gait in that he dragged his left leg slightly. Neil could not decide if it was an injury or the after effects of a stroke. Anyway, why was he here? He continued towards the car and Neil was about to switch the communications panel when he saw what he thought was an Uzi. Neil retracted the wing mirrors and waited, patiently, calmly and with his wits about him. The man tried to fire at the side window, a shoot that should have broken the glass and killed Neil. The bullets bounced off and flew around the carriage and one struck the man in the left arm. He let his grip of the weapon go and Neil turned the mirrors to out, which meant that they hit the man's right hand and the weapon fell to the floor of the train. Neil opened the back door and the man found himself trapped, stopped from running back the way he had arrived. The man was trying to grope for the weapon as Neil used immediate open on the window and punched him on the jaw. He fell hard against the car and Neil opened the door, which pushed him away from the vehicle, allowing Neil to get out. He had the Heckler in his hand and waited for the man to pick himself up.

"OK asshole what do you think you were going to do?" The man said nothing and Neil heard the movement behind him. Turning half way to see who had entered the carriage, he saw the chef. "Take this man and get the authorities to lock him up." Neil used the weapon's barrel to suggest that the man move around the car on the opposite side. The man started to move and then fell to his knees, blood and froth coming out of his mouth and his cheeks went cherry red. Neil walked across to the man who was, by now, in a coma and obviously dying from cyanide poisoning. "Don't worry about locking him up. Just tell the police in the UK what had happened and give them this card please." The card was for a senior official of the Foreign and Commonwealth Office (FCO) in London with a telephone number and nothing else. "You will be leaving the scene of a crime," said the chef. "Yes, I will be. That is why you need to give them this card."

The train came out of the tunnel. Neil got back into the car and waited to start the engine. His mind was racing; no one knew he was going by Eurotunnel, except the train staff. He would drive from Dover. The muck was getting deeper once more.

He turned to the official and said, "Tell the passengers that unloading will be delayed due to a passenger being taken ill in the front of the train." Neil dialled a six-digit number and requested police and an ambulance. "Open up my door and I will leave, the police will be here soon. You will need to make a statement, thanks for your help." Neil got back into the vehicle, started the engine and moved slowly forward as the doors started to open. He drove up the ramp and out of the terminal, turning to go through the VIP section and did not stop at the passport control. Well no one was in the booth anyway! He drove out on to the motorway and thought about stopping at the first services for a coffee and the call of nature. I see he thought to himself as he started weaving through the traffic. He looked at his watch and realised that he would need to get a move on to ensure that he made the meeting as he had promised. The sun was shining and he thought that everything looked clean as he drove towards London and the Ministry.

Neil had thought about stopping in Sidcup and getting the train. His communication's panel burst into life with a female voice saying to him, "Can you talk?" "Yes, who are you?" "I am the EA to the PS." Neil spoke slowly and calmly "OK stupid as it may sound to you. You are the executive assistant to the Permanent Secretary at which government department please. "I am sorry I can't give you more information. They said …" Neil switched the communication off and drove. His instinct was telling him that something was not right. He had no idea what was not right. Whatever it was, it was not right. Not very helpful he thought to himself. He rang a four-digit code and said, "I am back in the country and on my way to the Whitehall meeting. Anything I need to know?" The crisp reply was "No, good to have you back." Liar Neil thought and cut that discussion off. He had followed protocol and could get back to working out the best way to get to the meeting on time. He had passed the services; the call of nature would have to wait! Not the M25 go straight in to the centre of London.

He pulled over and jumped out of the vehicle, rang around the back and into some trees, by the roadside. He had to have a comfort break. He did not take long and was back in the driver's seat feeling better in no time. He eased back into the flow of traffic and looked at the moving map to confirm where he was. The EA to the PS came back on the line.

"Please don't hang up" she said. "Not to put too fine a point on it, who the hell are you and why do I need to talk with you. I'm busy right now." "Look you ass, I am ringing you because Sigs 2 said if he bought it, I was to get in touch and give you a message. Can you receive a classified message on this link?" Neil pushed a button and a male voice was talking to someone else. "OK now get out please this is highly classified. Neil it is me, I was set up for helping you. I recorded this before Kiev. Do not go to Vauxhall; do not trust Sir Joe, or his replacement. They are bringing back your mate Maurice from retirement to fill this desk. The Mandarins are out to get you. I do not know whom you turn to for help. They are going to kill you. They are scared that you know what is going to happen in the parts of the world you will have just left. They see you as too powerful, too much of an honest broker. That is why they wanted you to use the killing route home. Yes the killing route. I have to go. You are and always will be my friend." The transmission stopped and Neil closed the link before the girl could say anything. A car cut across him and he swore loudly. He watched as the car carried on weaving in and out the traffic. Trained police driver that one Neil thought to himself, you can always tell.

By now, Neil was in London traffic and he turned into Trafalgar Square and drove down towards Downing Street. He turned into the barrier opposite the MOD and showed his pass. "Sorry I need to park this here as well." The police officer nodded and the gates opened to let him in. He drove down the street and parked on the opposite side to number 10 and away from possible cameras. He spoke to the police officer at the end by the exit barrier. "Someone will come and pick this up soon, OK?" "Yes sir, but soon please." Neil pushed the switch that locked the car and put it into self-protection mode. He walked up to the door at number 12 and it opened as he approached. "Up the stairs and first floor on the right," he heard. Entering the meeting room, he apologised that he was a little late. Three men, one secretary, also male, and a woman sat around the table. Neil sat in the vacant wooden chair. He looked at the faces of the people around the table. George he knew from the department, the chair he did not know. He was not sure about the other man and the women could have been anyone, blue rinse and pearls. The secretary was a departmental man, he knew by sight.

The person acting as chair said, "I think introductions are in order, yes?" He went on by saying "I am Sir Joseph's replacement. You can call me Sir Martin. I run the department now that you work for Neil. We are here to sort out what happened. Why and what should we do. You know George, that is Erica and the gentleman opposite you is Claude." He had not let anyone introduce himself or herself and was busy moving papers around as he spoke. "Oh, I am glad that we got the introductions out of the way" Neil said sarcastically. "Where have you come from Sir Martin, the Ministry of Agriculture and Fisheries I suppose?"

"What do you mean?" Sir Martin looked up and was angry, His face was about to go red as he fought to control himself. "What I mean is that you have arrived from nowhere, no actual introduction from anyone around this table and you assume you have the right to be rude and obnoxious. That is what I mean. Do you understand me Sir Martin?"

"Who the hell do you think you are, coming in here like you are someone important and talking to me like that? Shut up, this instant." Neil of course did not shut up and turned to George, "You know that dad has gone this time, no hiding?" George nodded his head and looked at Sir Martin. Neil had successfully destroyed the meeting in a few phrases, George knew it and so did everyone around the table except Sir Martin. A slim, willowy man with thick black spectacles and a handmade suit. Grey in colour of course, but well-tailored and the waist cut in to accentuate his figure. Every inch a mandarin from somewhere in Whitehall. A petulant mandarin was this one.

Neil turned back to Sir Martin and said low and slow voice, "What did you do before this position please? Excuse me if I seem a little on edge. I have just returned from what should have been a milk run, which ended in me nearly being killed, my best friend being killed in Kiev, and my father being killed in Paris. Please excuse the tone of my comments. Putting it into simple straightforward language, who are you? Where do you come from and who appointed you?" Sir Martin drew himself up to his full height, remained seated and said, very quickly, "I was the PS at Ministry of Culture, Media and Sport!"

"Oh good, nice to know you have been appointed because you know something about the game." Neil had already had enough of this upstart, sorry "Ennobled upset." He went on, "Is this an inquest on the death of Sir Joseph or a witch hunt? Either way I am not mindful to put up with your claptrap. Either get to the point, allow everyone around the table to introduce themselves; I know the names now. I have another meeting to get to a few doors down this road."

Sir Martin, got up, grabbed his papers and turning to the secretary, he said, "This meeting is adjourned, now!" He walked out of the room trying to look dignified and failing completely. He uttered a small cough as he passed Neil, but did not cover his mouth.

Neil turned to George and said, "What happens now?" "You go to your next meeting I suppose." "That was a ruse. I need to go and see the quartermaster and get some stuff. Can you put in a leave pass for me please George about 3 weeks? I am going to Moscow and then China for a short break. I have to make a few calls, would you people mind leaving me in the room on my own please?" Everyone got up and left. Neil rang a number and said to no one in particular, "Tell the driver to meet me outside Number 10 Downing Street. Can they make it in about 30 minutes please?" He heard a mumbled yes and went on, "Nothing too flashy, black please and with darkened windows. Also, arrange for a meeting tonight in London of the senior members. Book a room at the Army and Navy in my name. OK?" The line went dead. Neil knew that it would all be arranged. He texted the membership number to the telephone number and sat back in his seat. *Well that had gone as badly as you ever hope it could go,* he thought to himself. Neil suddenly realised that he was tired, very tired. Tired of people trying to kill him, tired of Mandarins, who knew nothing and acted as if they did, tired of being on his own, and yes he was getting tired of his job. He got up and checked himself before he opened the door. He had been in this room before and decided to use the emergency exit rather than walk into something unpleasant through the door. It was an oak panelled door with a key in the locked. Neil locked the door and moved over the table where Sir Martin had been sitting. He lifted the telephone received that was in the chair arm and another door opened in the wall behind him. He walked carefully and closed this door slowly behind him. Waiting until his eyes became used to the light he then moved down the passageway and opened the door to his left. That let him onto the staircase from which he quickly descended and let himself out of the building. He could hear a noise as people were trying to get into the room he had just left.

Quartermaster and the Network. Then?

Chapter 15

Neil walked to the "back door" of Downing Street and the police officer on duty said, "Your car was picked up Sir." "Thank you. Don't worry I am about to be picked up; but, thank you for letting me know," Neil replied slowly and tried to calm down his breathing a little. Walking through the exit Neil turned to his right and started walking on the gravel of Horse Guards Parade. He was thinking and his phone ringing broke his thoughts. "Yes?" "Sir, I am your new driver and I was asked to pick you up. I saw you coming out of the back door and parked. This police officer is giving me a hard time and saying that I cannot stop here. Would you come over and explain to him that I am here to pick you up?" Neil looked across to his left and saw a black car and a police officer standing next to it, with his notebook out. Neil broke into a run and arrived at the side of the police officer as he heard him saying, "And who is so important that you can ignore the parking regulations?" "Me" said Neil and the police officer turned around. "And who might you be Sir, if I may be so bold to ask?" Neil took out his ID card and showed the police officer. "Oh! Sorry Sir, I did not know. The driver would not tell me anything except she was here for someone and she could park here. I did not mean to delay you." "Of course, not, you are doing your job. This is my new driver and … Well no harm done. I need to move sorry." Neil got into the rear seat and said to the driver, "Go up to the top and turn left and drive towards the Palace. Then turn left and come back up to Great George Street." The driver pulled off smoothly and Neil pushed a button on his phone. The phone speaker sounded in the car and he heard "Arthur's emporium and exchange stores. Your needs are our provisions, Arthur speaking, how can we help you?" "Arthur it's Neil, I need a new set of luggage. Do you have any ready now?" "Now Sir, do you mean now? May I just ask you a few questions to confirm that you are one of our regular customers? Do you have a client number Sir?" Arthur was waiting, but had recognised Neil's voice. He was punching up Neil's account on his terminal. Neil called a number that was exactly that shown on the computer. "Fine Sir, where would you like these items delivered please?" "How about the front of Portcullis House in 5 minutes?" Neil knew he was pushing his luck. "5 minutes is a little tight Sir. I am will dispatch the items now. Charged to your account. Please be aware that this is a new model. It fits together, please read the attached instructions, just in case. Any other requirements or instructions?" "Yes please confirm it is me in the black car and then place then items in the boot of the car." "Of course Sir, always a pleasure doing business with you. Will you be dropping in at any time soon?" Neil cut the connection. Albert had someone in his office. Someone was listening in and he had used the set code word.

Neil turned to the driver, "Go across Parliament Square and turn left and park in front of Portcullis house." The driver said nothing and just looked at the traffic. Pulling up in front of Portcullis, a police officer stepped forward. Neil waved his pass and pushed the button to wind down the window slightly. "Just collecting some items." The police officer looked about and saw someone coming towards the car with a set of luggage. "This one Sir?" "Yes" Neil looked at the man pulling the luggage; he was shaking his head and talking to himself. He shouted, "Put it in the back governor?" Neil nodded his head and the driver popped the trunk. Neil said to the driver, "Go for Hardwick Drive please?" They heard the trunk slam shut and the driver pulled away amid horns sounding as she pulled out without worrying about the oncoming traffic.

Neil sat back in the leather seats and asked "Can we get a coffee please, and will you call ahead to arrange a meeting of the board for the Network please?" "Left hand cabinet, only espresso. Yes I will call ahead now sir." They were travelling through London quickly and were already on the south side of the Thames. Neil pushed the catch, a small tray came out, and a hot espresso was poured into a china cup. Nice touch Neil thought. He slowly drank the hot coffee and enjoyed the flavour and the roast of the beans. His mind turned to the driver. He asked "How new are you and what should I call you please?" He could not tell too much looking at the back of her head and shoulders. Good shoulders a well cut suit and clean and tidy hair, pageboy style. She could drive and that was important to Neil. She did not turn her head as she replied. "I am Gloria and I have been with the Network for about 3 years. I only drive for number one, anywhere, anytime. I am your driver and you can always get me on any mobile if you dial +77 001109." She was passing the traffic with ease and the journey was going quickly.

Neil's phone rang and he answered it. "Where are you and what the hell do you think you were doing at the meeting this morning? Who do you think you are? I don't appreciate my staff being made to look stupid in any type of meeting!" "I did not make him look stupid; he did that on his own." Neil poured himself another espresso and sighed aloud. "Don't get smart with me young man. I will cast you off and leave you with nowhere to go. I can do that." "If you need to tell me that, then you cannot do it. Stop blustering and get on with what you need to tell me please, I am on my way to an important meeting." "How dare you! How dare you, you young upstart!" "I am certain that I am speaking with PS for SIS, Sir Joseph's brother, Frederic. So please stop blustering and get to the point or I will cut the call. I am sorry for your loss," Neil lied. He was not sorry that the old number one was dead. The fact that he wanted his father dead was enough for Neil to feel that way. The fact that he had ordered his father death was another reason. The final act that his father was dead was just too much. He turned the phone off and drank his espresso, which was going cold. He wondered if Frederic knew that he, Neil, had killed his brother. He did not care. He turned his mind to the meeting in Hardwick Drive. He was then to be en route to Russia and thence China to see his stepmother. Things that, to Neil, were much more important an overweight civil servant who was a pain in the rectum. He thought about the hand off the luggage. Why was Alfred so worried? Who was in the room when they were talking? Either had the people trying to kill him stopped, or was he wrong again. He looked up and saw that they were turning into Hardwick Drive. That was quick! He pushed the button but did not get a response from Albert's emporium. That was odd. He tried again and still nothing. "Drive into the garage and wait before we go down to the parking area please." Neil had said this without thinking. He wanted time to think and the garage was as good a place as anywhere was. Gloria, sat still and quiet whilst the doors of the garage shut down and she hit the lock button inside in the car. Neil poured his third espresso and slowly drank the hot, flavoursome coffee. "What is this brew please Gloria?" "Special to our, sorry, your organisation." Gloria switched the video on and then apologised. "No leave it on please Gloria."

Neil looked at the screen and panned through the cameras. Nothing and no one, that was odd, too odd. "Please activate the computer for this screen and get us out of here now Gloria." Neil knew that the front garage door was a fake, a force field and a cardboard door, which gave anyone who touched it a shock. Gloria did not question his words, just drove the car through the cardboard door, having switched off the force field. Neil punched in "Evac code Bravo" and "Bugout Alpha" on the computer keyboard.

Gloria pulled the car out of the gateway and drove straight across the road into the side street. She knew the drive and headed for the South Circular Road and towards the safe house related to code Bravo. "You know that I checked this out last week on behalf of number three!" "No I did not know. Is it still safe?" "Yes I think so, no one had been there for ages, dust and grim everywhere." Neil sat back and said nothing. Replies came up on the computer screen confirming that the evac had taken place and the meeting had been transferred to the new safe house. The code meant no cars, walk to the house and everyone that had responded had agreed, except number three. The new number three. Neil typed in the request for details on number three and the computer asked for a security code. He asked Gloria for the code and she asked him how he knew the evac codes and bugout call? "I have been doing a little reading in my spare time. But not enough it seems." She typed in the code as she skilfully drove the care through the south London traffic. The electronic file appeared on Neil's screen and he took time to read it carefully.

The new number three was a thirty year old, Oxford first in Classics, short service commission in the Guards and recently recruited into the SIS. His father Sir Joseph had recruited him into the Network. "Oh Shit!" Neil exclaimed without thinking. "Sorry Sir, is there a problem?" "Yes I think so Gloria, pull over when you can please. Find a quiet coffee shop or café." "It's not the best place Sir." "Just find somewhere please Gloria."

Neil's telephone rang and he answered it. "Albert here, can't talk, don't use the suitcases, I will get you clean ones soon." He was gone. As the car pulled up, Neil jumped out and took the cases from the trunk. He placed them next to the café wall, said to Gloria, "Drive around for 10 minutes, then come back, and see if the suitcases are gone." Neil set off in the direction of a sweet shop, not the café. He crossed the road at the traffic lights and headed for the petrol station, which he knew, was just down the road on the left hand side. He entered the shop and said to the man behind the counter, "My battery is out have you got a phone I can use?" The man replied, "Only if you can pay for it!" "Yes, I can; but, I will need a receipt." The man did not look up and pushed a button on the panel at his side. A door opened and he waved for Neil to go in. The password was correct. He sat down in a small room with a telephone, coffee makings and no windows. He got out his mobile and pushed to speak with Gloria. "Please pick me up from the petrol station just down the road from the café, just drive on to the forecourt and I will see you in the camera." He cut of the communication and looked around the room. To the trained eye, it was a cheap and cheerless, staff room, with not much in it in terms of staff comforts. Neil pulled open the wooden draw of the table in front of him and took out what looked like a TV hand control. He pushed the power button and the wall next to the door revealed a bank of TV and computer screens. Neil could now see the forecourt, a log of calls being made, or had been made by his mobile and the man outside. He waited for the computer keyboard to rise up from the table's surface. He needed time to think and sort things out in his mind. However, he did not have that luxury at present. He typed in the address for his private emails and quickly looked at the list of unread messages. He needed time to think, to sort things into some order before the meeting. Nothing of real importance he thought as he glanced at the list. Then one message caught his eye. It was from a "qq" address and was not from anyone he recognised. He was about to delete the message as he always did, when something stopped him. He checked that the mail was clean of virus and attachments, and then opened it. It was from his father's wife, Gui. "Can you visit and please speak with me urgently?" It had come from Qingdao and a telephone number was all that was written, nothing else! More problems or concerns. He still needed to sort out tonight's meeting and get to Moscow, before he could fly to China. He saw Gloria's car pull up and park over behind the pumps and not close to the road. She could wait a minute. His mobile rang and he looked at the screen to see the private number for the QM.

Albert came on the line. "Neil can you talk, I am clear now?" He did not wait for a response and just carried on. "Someone doesn't like you a lot. I mean a lot. It was a set up and the case should have exploded by now, killing you. I have put a clean set of luggage in your safe box at Sydenham station. You know what I mean. Be careful! Do not take calls from the new boss; I will get Maurice to contact you soon. He is in post now and like me is worried for your neck." Albert broke off and put the telephone down. The line cut off and Neil was even more confused than before. He closed everything down and opened the door to the petrol station. He nodded thanks to the man and walked out, picking up a mars bar without paying. "Next time," the man shouted and Neil shouted back, "If there is a next time." He walked to the car and saw Gloria looking around, seemingly wondering where he was.

She was visibly shaken. "It exploded, just as I was about to drive off. It exploded, you were walking down the road, I was checking to move out into the traffic, and the case exploded. It took the front of the café out. Why?" Neil did not answer he sat back in the seat and said, "Drive to Sydenham please use the South Circular and turn left at the traffic lights for Sydenham." Gloria drove off the forecourt and concentrated on the traffic. She turned the car into the traffic went up to the lights and turned left just before the police stopped all of the traffic as a fire engine arrived. Gloria drove past Eltham Palace and towards the dual carriageway and then the South Circular. Neil used the time to think. Well to try to think.

He needed to check who else was with number 3. He needed to pick up a set of luggage and then book some tickets for flights. *The night flight to Moscow should be safe enough* he thought to himself. *Who in the department was gunning for him now?*

Maurice's voice disturbed his train of thought, "What are you up to you old rascal?" It was code word to say that he was alone and the line was clear to talk. "I am on my way to a meeting and trying not to get myself killed. I thought I had cleared all that up. Obviously not! How is your family these days?" Maurice cleared his throat and Neil knew that something had changed. "Thank you for the briefing Sigs 2, I will take care and get in touch when my plane lands in Moscow bye." Neil hung up.

Maurice however, had turned to see a thin, tall man walk into the office and stand by his desk. "May I take the liberty of asking who you are and what is your clearance might to be in here?" "Good afternoon, Maurice, I am the new department head, the one that Neil was told to be careful off. My name is Stone. We need to talk. Here is a good a place as any. May I sit down?" Maurice pushed out a chair for the man to sit down and thought to himself, shit I have not even had my chair warm and the intrigue is already getting too much. He looked at the man full face. Ice blue eyes and a square chin, good tailored suit and polished loafers. A tie he could not place and a white cotton shirt with a Prince of Wales collar. Maurice was not one to judge, but … "Seal the door, I am not armed Maurice." It was not a request it was an order. A retired Group Captain Maurice was not taking kindly to orders by a plain grey suit, no rank or title. Maurice locked the door from his seat and set the tempest switch to on. Nothing and no one would hear this conversation, except the two people in this room and his tape recorder working in his draw. Better safe than sorry he had thought and had switched it on as he had moved to the switch panel using his back to cover his action. The thin man put his hand into his packet and pulled out a micro recorder, which he switched off. "Would you mind doing the same please Maurice?" "What do you mean?" Maurice asked blankly. "As I can't see anything in your pockets, I must assume the recorder is in your draw. Please switch it off, please!" The last please was odd and Maurice, reluctantly agreed, opened the draw and put his micro recorder onto the desk. He switched it off. Turned slowly to the man, he said equally slowly, "What can I do for you and why are you here?"

"My name is of no importance, who I work for is similar to Neil, although on paper he works for me. You can call me Frederick for now. Neil is in grave danger." "When isn't he?" Maurice added. "Until he gets to his meeting he is in grave danger, at the meeting I can help him. You need to do a few things for me and accept that I can order you and will get the PM to approve my orders. Alternatively, you can trust me and do as I ask. The latter is a better route for helping Neil."

Maurice sat and thought through what he had said. The thin man did not speak for a while. "What meeting are you talking about? Who the hell are you and what is your interest in this whole bloody mess?" Maurice was not sure what to say or do. He had no way of checking what the man, Frederick, had said or was liable to say.

Frederick's face changed slightly to reflect his frustration that Maurice was not sure of him. "I'm telling you the truth. Neil is on his way to a meeting and he needs help. He is in grave danger!" Maurice replied again, "He is always in danger, which is his job to sort out other's peoples mess and put things right. Well back to normal if, he can. He is very good at what he does. So why is he in any more danger than usual?"

Frederick moved uncomfortably in his chair. "What is your security clearance now Maurice?" "What the hell has that got to do with anything? I have do not know who you are, what you do, or any evidence to support your claims. I do not really know what you are doing here, asking for a special chat. Why should I listen to you anymore? I have not a single idea what you are trying to achieve here?"

Frederick sat up straight and tore back with his view of the world. "You need to believe me; I have a vested interest in keeping Neil alive. I promised his father before he died. You never knew his father did you. He was a brilliant operative. He died saving Neil. I was trained by him and promised to keep an eye on Neil if he died. He is dead. I belong to the same organisation of which Neil has just taken control. This organisation has nothing to do with his daytime job, and everything to do with world peace. I know what is happening before the meeting and I must, will attend this evening. You know more than you need to and I think we had better get you into the organisation for your own safety and that of your loved ones."

Maurice could not help himself he blurted out, "Bollocks!" Frederick smiled and replied, "I said that myself when I was introduced to the network. I imagine Neil said the same."

Gloria was walking around the hypermarket and was remembering the checking of the safe house. Number three was her man and she loved him; but she was not happy about his idea to kill her new boss. Neil was a nice man! *What a terrible English word "nice,"* she thought. *It meant nothing, why should number 3 kill number 1, he had seen his father murdered, because "a father could not and would not kill his son." What was nice about that?* Gloria, inadvertently found herself smoothing her dress when she thought of number one. He was good looking and had something that attracted women. Well attracted her at least. Yet she was in love with number 3. She strolled up the isles and looking at the food on the shelves. Her phone bleeped and she was surprised that it was Number one. She had been thinking about him and wondered if he had been thinking about her. "I am taking the car, please walk up to the meeting. It is not far and the weather is fine." The phone cut off. She did not like the idea of Neil off on his own when he was in danger. Gloria felt responsible!

The support staff were arriving at the safe house for the meeting and instructions had been given and followed. Calmly and quietly around the back of the shops in the High Street, people took their places. The chain across the entry to the safe house had been removed and placed carefully on the ground so that no one would fall and hurt himself or herself. Personal weapons were being checked and put back into holsters. Eyes were on the roof of the old post office and a road sweeper was cleaning the same part of the road across from the entrance. Inside the safe house, doors were being checked for locked or open as required. The room was checked for packages that should not be there and things that should be where they are required. Number three was already onsite and supervising everything. He had arrived before the external guards. He had taken Gloria's recommendation and not put the gun under the desk and had used double-sided sticky back tape to hold the gun in front of his seat, but facing number one's chair, with the handle to the side. He felt comfortable and ready. He dismissed the support team and sat down at his place at the end of the table. The table had name cards placed on the positions for the "guests." Eight seats, one at the head of the table with his at the bottom and three each side. Number 3 did not know who was going to attend; he was going to ensure that Number one sat at the head of the table so he could avenge his father's death.

Gloria started to walk up the High Street in bright sun light, passed poor looking shops and food outlets. She felt good in the sun, but worried about her new boss. She strolled slowly, the worry was not enough to make her change her pace or do anything except think about what could be, or even what might be if things were different.

Maurice and Frederick got up, took their jackets, and went out from the office together. Maurice called his number 2 and said, "Take control and I will not be on call for the next few hours." Frederick simply said to his aid, who was hovering, "Get the car please." The aid was a thickset man with a tight suit. He was not a civil servant by the look of him.

Neil had parked the car in the public car park and walked up to the local gym and swimming pool. He had shown his company member ship card and had walked through the turnstiles after he had bought a pair of swimming trunks from reception. He was sitting in the sauna and thinking in peace and quiet. A couple of old women were swimming and a fat man was in the Jacuzzi. He was really fed up with people trying to blow him up, attack him, shoot him and generally trying to get rid of him. He did not mind in the field, but at home on his own turf. That was a bit too much. He slowly put the pieces together; there was a leak in the Sigs group. Too many people knew where he was and when.

The rules for the Network needed to be looked at, concerning killing and being killed. Someone was trying to stop him getting to China now. The meeting needed to discuss the problem of Russia and the Ukraine, which was coming to a boil. Funny that he had been routed through the Ukraine just before the troubles started to come to the surface. He needed to sort out the Russian end, as the man who had come to murder him was one of his staff from overseas. Finally, he had to visit China and see what his father had been doing. He sat up in the sauna, put his feet on the floor, and stretched. He loved the heat and his body felt good. His body had been taking some punishment of late. The sauna felt good. Unfortunately no massage. Still another time. He still had to sort out the number three problem. He went into the showers and washed in warm water, dried himself and dressed. If he had suitcases, he would have changed his underwear and socks. No such luck! He would pick up a new set before the flight to Moscow in the early hours. He mused, that he must leave enough time to get to the airport. It was all coming to a head, or was it? Neil said to himself as he slowly walked up the stairs from the pool and the sauna, *I feel fine for a change, marvellous what a sauna and a few moments on your own could do for the body and the mind.* Neil then realised that he had put his weapon in the car before he went to the gym. He walked back towards the High Street and the car park. He would go to the meeting tooled up, just in case.

Things Will Come to a Climax

Chapter 16

Neil had just closed and locked the car. He had put on his should holster and slid the gun into place before he noticed Gloria walking towards the car. She looked good, a little warm from walking in the sun. A firm body and curves where they ought to be. She was fit! Neil spoke first. "You should have gone straight to the meeting?" "I always want to know where the car is exactly in case of trouble. "Are you expecting trouble?" "You can never be too sure, are you?" "Yes!" Gloria was just a little too close to him and he could smell the perfume. He could not resist. "Channel number five, yes?" She seemed even closer, if that were possible, without their bodies touching. Neil excited her and cause feelings she had not felt for a very long time. "How about dinner at the airport after the meeting?" "Are you propositioning me?" "Offering dinner' anything else is up to you!" Neil was teasing and she was flirting. They were both attracted to each other, but this was the main car park and many people were coming and going. He touched her hand and that would have to do, until he could kiss her. His touch sent electricity up her hand and arm. She pushed forward that last little bit and kissed his cheek, softly, yet with passion. She pulled away and there was a tear on her cheek. "I am supposed to kill you Neil. Nevertheless, I cannot. I want you and want to be with you." She blurted this out before her common sense could stop her. Neil automatically stood back from her. "Well that would be terminal and cause a stir at the meeting. Number three would then assume number one's position as you would nominate him to take my place." "I cannot do it, I just cannot! Even if you don't want me, I can't!"

"Get in the car and stay there please Gloria." Spoken softly and quietly it was an order not a request. She did as she was told and sat in the driver's seat, and started to cry. Neil walked away and up to the High Street. He walked to the new looking traffic lights, crossed the High Street, and walked towards the railway station not the safe house.

Frederick and Maurice were fighting their way through London traffic and both looked worried, in case they were late. They could not be.

Neil's telephone rang, he answered after he had looked at the number. Русский голос "встреча создана, оружие под столом. Не сидите на вершине. Будет видеть вас в Москве." (A Russian voice said, "The meeting is a set-up, gun under the table. Do not sit at the top. Will see you in Moscow."). Neil hung up and sighed. More questions about how people knew. He walked slowly towards the station entrance. Anyone watching would assume that he was going to the station; he slipped into the alley and walked quickly towards the end, as he took out his weapon and checked the magazine. He put the gun back in the holster and stopped at the end of the alley. He looked across to the old post office and saw the man on the roof. He raised his hand and the man waved and ducked back behind the chimneys. A man walked towards Neil from the entrance alley and again Neil raised his hand. The man was smiling. "Hello boss how are you? Number three has not come in. Well I have not seen him sir." "Don't worry, just be ready I will need you to drive me later."

They walked across the road and down the alley to the back door entrance. He stopped and said to the driver "No I will go another way." Neil turned around and walked back to the road, turned left and walked on to the High Street. He went into the shop below the meeting room and smiled at the owner. He gave the password and walked to the back of the shop. He touched a panel and opened a door inside the shop that entered the hallway of the flats. He checked and saw that the camera was facing the entry door not where he was standing.

Maurice and Frederick arrived in the road and jumped from the car. Driver stopped them and asked for ID. Frederick showed his pass and said, "He is with me, hurry up, and has number one arrived?" "I haven't seen him entered the building," Driver partly lied.

Gloria had left the car and walked to the entrance; Driver checked her ID and joked with her about being late. She moved like a big cat up the stairs and into the meeting room. Number one's chair was empty and there was a man she did not know sitting next to number two. Two people had not turned up and the scribe was reading the minutes of the last meeting. She sat down next to the scribe who looked at her a little surprised. He finished reading and said, "We should declare before number one turns up. May I remind you all that a declaration is required and must be observed?" Number three said, "No, we should wait for number one." That would allow him to kill number one. Number two asked had the scribe heard from number one, as he appeared to be late. The scribe looked up and replied, "He will be here, and of that there is no doubt."

Neil sat down after closing the door and was shocked to see that his hands were shaking. He had been in many tight spots. So why was he scared now? He had survived murder attempts. Was he still viewed as an honest broker for many nations? He hoped so. Was one of his employers out to get him? He was one of very few agents that had this title of an honest broker between nations. Should he just get up and walk away from the Network? He was exhausted and fought to control himself. Simply put, he had to walk into a room and risk being killed. Had they take the declaration? Who had turned up? This house had been chosen because it was so difficult to get into it without being seen, cameras, guards, doors and stairs. He drank the remains of a black coffee the shopkeeper had brought him. He felt better as the hot liquid seemed to fill his body and allow his confidence to return. He must not allow that to happen again; otherwise, he ought to give up and that would be the end. Had his father died for him to give up? No! He had a job to do, his job, his way of earning his living, his way of making a difference in a world. He pushed the button on the wall that looked like a light switch. It opened the cupboard that had looked like a piece of furniture for sale.

Neil looked at the monitor to see who was on the stairs. He took a white coat and put some bits and pieces in to his pockets, some gas bomb pellets, four, and an oxygen breather. This was small and fitted into the mouth, a bit like a gum shield. He took throwing knives. Three triangles, these were razor sharp and flew like the Chinese star throwing knives. No gun! He also took out a small multi meter. He was formulating a plan. Go up as a technician and gain access to the complex that way. He was not sure that this would work. He was not sure of anything, except that he did not want to die here and now.

The meeting was stalling and no one was talking. The impasse over declaration had upset the scribe. He was not aware of the hidden agenda or gun that number three had. Number three thought the agenda shared by Gloria. Gloria was in a turmoil, as she did not want number one or number three killed. She could not see a way out of the problem. Number two was tapping his foot. He had broken the rules and brought a gun in his brief case, which was on the table. Scribe kept asking him to put the case on the floor.

Gloria said slowly and calmly, "I have killed number one. He will not be arriving, and as such I give up the seat to number three." She had done what she had promised to Sir Joseph's son. Number two got up and started shouting at her calling her a bitch and a traitor. Maurice got up and did not know what to do. He stood by the windows and decided to move out onto the balcony. Had he failed to support Neil as he had hoped? The scribe was banging the table and number three was pushing his chair and starting to stand up. Whilst all this was going on Neil slipped into the room and moved into the kitchen area; appearing to ignore what was happening. Gloria got up and as she passed number three, she used her nails to cut the back of his hand. The poison would work soon. She wanted number one. She apologised and number three said, "No problem, just a nick." Gloria sat in number three seat, number two was still on his feet and number three sat in number one's seat. "Please all sit down and shut up." Number three was now acting as if he was number one. Neil wanted to turn around and stop him, but his instinct told him to wait. Everyone seemed to calm down; Maurice was on the balcony and did not move to come back into the room. Number three now looked up and asked whom the technician in the side area was and what were they doing. Neil did not reply or turn around. The scribe said, if this state of affairs is true, you need to explain to the committee what you did and why and then we can declare. The scribe was that unflappable. Number two was busy opening his briefcase and had pulled it close to him. Suddenly the scribe said as if it was an afterthought, "We are not quorate. We can't do anything." Number three said, "I don't care, if people did not turn up, it does not matter. I am in charge now." Neil thought he was very sure of himself even though the action to declare had not happened. His instinct told him to sit tight and continue to fiddle with something on the side.

Neil knew that the scribe was getting irate and heard him tell number three to shut up as no one had confirmed any death, yet. Number two had managed to pull out his plastic gun from his case and levelled it at number three. He did not say anything just pulled the trigger and watched as red hole appeared in his forehead. The he said, "I was related to Sir Joseph as much as you were; but, we needed a change. Neil was that change!" He sat down. Maurice went to move into the room, when he saw that Gloria had somehow also pulled a gun. She aimed it at number two and as she had been trained, she pulled the trigger. Number two died before he had been able to sit down. He fell to the floor. This was becoming a blood bath. Neil was on the verge of turning around when he heard the door open. He turned to look, but could not see anything as the wall obscured the entrance. Instinct made him press the panic and the escape hatch buttons. The scribe turned around and a look of fear came across his face. Gloria turned around and was face to face with the dead Sir Joseph. Neil still did not know who had entered the room. Before he could say or do anything, the man said, "The time has come to cleanse the Network." Gloria saw that he has his coat open and had a string of plastic explosive strapped to his waist. Without a single additional word, he pushed the button and the room exploded! For Neil the room went black and the whole world went black as the building collapsed around him.

Driver, who was outside, could not believe what had happened. He had not seen anyone else come in or go out. He ran towards where the backdoor had been and tried to force an entry. Rubble, brick, and no way into the building. He ran back to his team of guards and shouted for them to follow him. They all ran to the front of the shop. Driver started to throw bricks and stone pieces behind him, causing more chaos as traffic had come to an abrupt halt. His job was to find and save number one. He must find him and get him away from all this mess immediately.

Printed in Great Britain
by Amazon